BLACKMAILED DOWN THE AISLE

BLACKMAILED DOWN THE AISLE

BY

LOUISE FULLER

MILLS BOON

First published in Great Britain 2017
By Mills & Boon, an imprint of HarperCollins*Publishers*
1 London Bridge Street, London, SE1 9GF

Large Print edition 2017

© 2017 Louise Fuller

ISBN: 978-0-263-07136-8

Our policy is to use papers that are natural, renewable
and recyclable products and made from wood grown
in sustainable forests. The logging and manufacturing
processes conform to the legal environmental regulations
of the country of origin.

Printed and bound in Great Britain
by CPI Antony Rowe, Chippenham, Wiltshire

To my parents.
For taking me to the library. A lot.
Thank you.

CHAPTER ONE

THE PARTY WAS loud and hot and crowded.

Everywhere people were dancing, laughing, punching the air. Everyone was having fun. Everyone except Daisy Maddox. Leaning against the wall, her blonde hair lit up by the flashing strobe lights, she stood slightly apart, gazing critically across the room.

Nowhere in the world was as vibrant as Manhattan at midnight. And nowhere was more glamorous than Fleming Tower, the lean, gleaming skyscraper of steel and glass owned by her brother David's boss, Rollo Fleming, billionaire property tycoon and the party's host.

Daisy sighed softly. It was a great party.

As long as you were a guest!

Stifling a yawn, she glanced down at her uniform. If, like her, you were handing out glasses of champagne, then it was just another shift at work. And being a waitress sucked—no matter how cool the venue. Or how attractive the guests.

She glanced over at the young man who had been hovering at her elbow all evening.

Skinny, dark and charming, he was exactly her type. Ordinarily she might have flirted a little, but tonight she was struggling even to remember he was there.

'Come on!' He smiled at her hopefully. 'One little glass won't hurt.'

Behind his back, Joanne, another of the waitresses, rolled her eyes.

Daisy breathed out slowly. Six months ago she'd arrived at David's apartment, hoping to make it big on Broadway. Only just like the rest of her life nothing had gone to plan, and her dreams had got lost in a depressing loop of auditions and rejections. But all those years at drama school hadn't been entirely wasted, she thought wearily as, setting her expression to one of disappointment, she gave him a small, regretful smile.

'It's sweet of you, Tim. But I can't. Like I told you earlier. I don't drink when I'm working.' She glanced pointedly down at her uniform, but he wasn't taking no for an answer.

'It's not Tim—it's Tom. Come on. It's just one glass. I promise I won't tell.' He grinned encouragingly. 'It's not like the big boss man is here to catch you.'

Rollo Fleming. The 'big boss man.' Picturing his cool, handsome face—the one that gazed so disdainfully out from the Fleming Organisation's website—Daisy felt her heart thump nervously. It was true. Despite the fact that the party was in *his* building, for *his* staff, Rollo had declined to attend.

Of course, there had been the usual rumours he would turn up unannounced. Someone even claimed to have seen him in the foyer. But Daisy knew for sure that he wasn't coming. Rollo Fleming was in Washington on business, and by the time he returned the party would be wrapped up. Finished. Over.

And not just the party, she thought, glancing furtively at the clock on the wall.

'So do you work for him?'

Startled, she turned and saw that Joanne was looking curiously at Tom.

He nodded. 'Yeah, for about a year now.'

'Really?' Joanne's eyes widened. 'He is seriously hot. What's he like?'

Her question was directed at Tom, but Daisy had to bite her tongue to stop herself from replying. Hours scouring the internet had turned her into the world's leading authority on Rollo Fleming. Not that there was much to know. He rarely gave interviews and, aside from being photographed with a string of breathtakingly beautiful models and socialites, his private life was largely undocumented.

Tom shrugged, and a mixture of awe and admiration crossed his face. 'I don't have that much to do with him personally. But when it comes to business he's definitely got the Midas touch. *And* he gets all the hottest babes.'

He frowned.

'He's kinda scary too though. I mean, he works insanely hard and he's a total control freak. He knows everything that's going on—and I mean every tiny detail. And he's obsessed with honesty...' He paused, frowning. 'I was in a meeting with him once and there was a problem. Someone tried to cover it up and he was... Let's just say you wouldn't want to get on the wrong side of him.'

Daisy felt her stomach twist.

Tom's words confirmed everything David had already told her. Rollo Fleming was a ruthless workaholic and a commitment-phobic philanderer. Basically a supercharged version of Nick, her ex, and exactly the kind of man she loathed.

Looking up, her heart gave a jolt—not at the

memory of her latest failed relationship but at the time showing on the clock. Her shift was nearly over. On any other evening she would have been relieved, but tonight was different. Tonight was the first and hopefully the last time she would have to choose between breaking a promise and breaking the law.

'Are you okay?' Joanne nudged her arm. 'You look like you're going to be sick.'

Daisy swallowed. She felt as if she was too. Just thinking about what she was about to do was making the contents of her stomach curdle.

She smiled weakly. 'I know it's the city that never sleeps, but sometimes I wish New York would have an early night!'

'Look…' Glancing around, Joanne lowered her voice. 'Why don't you go home? I can finish up here.'

Daisy shook her head. 'I'm just tired. And I don't want to leave you in the lurch—'

'You're not!' Joanne frowned. 'So stop pretending you feel okay.'

Daisy hesitated. She hated lying to Joanne, particularly when her friend was being so kind. But she could hardly tell her the truth. She was only just coming to terms with it herself.

Stomach tightening, she thought back to the moment four days ago when she'd arrived back at David's apartment to find him in tears. After much coaxing he'd finally confessed that he had a gambling problem. *Only it was way more than a problem*. It turned out he'd been gambling and losing money for months, and his debt had spiralled out of control.

Daisy shivered. Her parents had drummed into them the importance of living within their means. But David's debt was the least of his problems. Dropping off some papers in Rollo Fleming's office earlier that day, he had noticed a watch on the floor. Only it hadn't been just *any* watch. It had been an exclusive designer watch. And he hadn't just noticed it. He'd picked it up and pocketed it, imagining that he'd be able to sell it and thus clear his debt.

Back home, he'd realised what he'd done and broken down completely. Which was why Daisy had ended up promising to return it for him.

The thought jogged her back into real time. Looking up, she grimaced. 'I do feel a bit odd. Maybe I will go now. Thanks, Jo. You're a star.'

Joanne nodded. 'Yes, I am. But don't be too grateful. I need you to cover for me on Tuesday.'

Her face softened. 'Cam's taking me out to dinner. It's our six-month anniversary.'

That was what she wanted to be doing, Daisy thought dully as she negotiated a path between the drunken partygoers into the deserted hallway. Going on an anniversary date with a boyfriend.

But, of course, that would require a boyfriend.

And five weeks ago Nick had decided that he needed some space.

Space!

Glumly, she stopped in front of the lifts.

Romeo never told Juliet he needed 'space.'

Antony hadn't said, 'It's not you, it's me,' to Cleopatra.

She stared at her reflection in the gleaming steel doors.

All men were unreliable and selfish or, more likely, she was just an extremely poor judge of character. Either way, she'd had enough. For the foreseeable future she was going to enjoy being single.

Reaching into the large pocket at the front of her apron, she pulled out a laminated card and stared down at her brother's face. Thank goodness for David. He was always there for her—helping her rehearse for auditions, even finding her this wait-ressing job.

Swiping the card, she felt her breath twitch in her throat as the light turned green and the doors slid open smoothly.

She owed David big time.

And now she had a chance to pay him back.

Her fingers trembled. But could she do it. Could she actually go through with it?

She hesitated. But only for a moment.

David was waiting downstairs for her in the lobby and the thought of his face, his relief as she walked towards him, propelled her forward.

Inside the lift, panicky thoughts fluttered inside her head, darting back and forth like startled birds, but then the doors were opening and, heart pound-ing, she stepped into a dimly lit corridor.

David had told her which office belonged to Rollo and, her heels clicking lightly on the pol-ished wood floor, she walked across the reception area and came to a standstill in front of a plain wooden door. For a moment she stared at it in si-lence. There was no nameplate—nothing to dif-ferentiate it from any of the other doors—and for a moment she wondered why. It seemed a strangely modest touch from a man worth billions who made no secret of the fact that he considered himself not just a businessman but an empire builder.

But then, did a man like Rollo Fleming really *need* any introduction? Particularly in the gleaming glass tower that bore his name.

It felt like she was about to enter the lion's den. But, lifting her chin, she braced her shoulders. The lion wasn't at home. And by the time he returned, she would be long gone.

Breathing in sharply, she swiped the card and pushed open the door.

Everything was silent and dark. But through the window all the familiar landmarks were lit up against the night sky, and she gazed at it in wonder. Rollo Fleming must have the best view in New York. But every moment spent in his office increased her risk of being caught and, galvanised by that thought, she stepped forward unthinkingly.

'Ouch!'

Her knee collided sharply with something hard in the darkness, but her pain was quickly forgotten as she felt whatever it was she'd walked into start to move. Heart pounding, she reached out, groping blindly, trying to stop whatever it was from falling. But it was too late, and the next moment there was a thump that echoed round the empty office like cannon fire.

'Good one, Daisy!' she muttered into the taut, strained silence that followed. 'Why don't you just set off some fireworks while you're at it?'

Gritting her teeth, she reached down and gingerly rubbed her knee—and then suddenly froze as from the other side of the door she heard the clear and unmistakable sound of footsteps approaching.

They slowed and stopped, and her heart began to beat with such force that she thought it would burst through her ribcage, and then she scrunched up her eyes as the door swung open and light flooded the room.

For the longest moment she waited—hoping, praying like a child that if she couldn't see whoever it was, they wouldn't be able to see her. But her hope was swiftly extinguished as a voice—cool, curt and very, very male—interrupted the tense silence.

'I've had a long and disappointing day, so I hope, for your sake, that you have a good explanation for this intrusion—'

Opening her eyes, Daisy blinked. The words had sent a ripple of dread down her spine, but that was nothing compared to the dismay she felt as she gazed up at the face of the man standing in front of the open door.

Rollo Fleming was supposed be in Washington.

On business.

But, unless she was hallucinating, neither of those facts were true.

The shock should have felled her and it would have done so, had she not been so distracted by the reality of his beauty.

On a screen, or in a magazine, Rollo Fleming was movie star handsome. In the flesh, however, his good looks were multiplied by ten, compounded by an intense mix of masculinity and power that made heat break out over her skin.

Not that he was her type, she thought hurriedly. He was too blonde, too poised, too calculating. It must just be the shock that was making her want to look at him. And keep on looking.

Golden-skinned, with a sharp clean-lined jaw and close-cropped blonde hair, he looked more like a Roman gladiator than a billionaire property tycoon. Only the very dark and obviously very expensive single-breasted suit gave any hint that he was worth more than the GDP of some small countries.

He looked at her directly then, and she felt

his gaze like cool water hitting the back of her throat. His eyes were extraordinary—clear, glittering green, like shards of broken glass. But it was the beautiful full-lipped curve of his mouth that tugged the most at her senses. It was a mouth she could imagine softening into the sexiest smile—

Her heart jerked.

Only it wasn't smiling now. Instead it was set in a straight, forbidding line that perfectly matched the rigid hostility of his body blocking the doorway. Nervously she glanced around the office, looking for another means of escape. But despite it being the size of a small barn, there were no other exits. Just a lot of cool designer-looking furniture.

She was trapped.

Her pulse shivered. This wasn't supposed to be happening. She hadn't come here for confrontation or explanation. But now there was no choice but to improvise.

'I—I can explain,' she stammered.

'Then I suggest you begin.'

He stood like an actor on stage, his spotlit face impassive, but there was a dangerous undertone in his voice that made her heartbeat accelerate unevenly.

'Just keep it short and simple. Like I said, I've had a long day… *Daisy*.'

He spoke her name softly, almost like an endearment, so that it was a moment before her brain registered the fact that he knew who she was. As she glanced up, eyes widening in shock, he shook his head dismissively, his gaze dropping to the laminated badge pinned to her blouse.

'So it *is* your name. I thought you'd stolen that from some poor hapless waitress downstairs.'

There was no mistaking the flicker of scorn in his eyes, and her hand rose protectively to cover the badge even as his accusation stung her out of her fear and shock.

'I didn't. My name really is Daisy and, for your information, I *am* one of those *poor hapless waitresses*. That's why I'm here.'

Her eyes locked with his. Pushing her hands into the pocket of her apron, her fingers brushed against David's security card, and she felt a sudden fierce urgency to protect her brother.

'I was working at the party downstairs and I was going to get some more napkins from the kitchens,' she lied. 'But I pressed the wrong button in the lift.'

For a moment Rollo stared at her coldly, then without turning he pushed the door shut.

In less than three seconds he had crossed the room, and as he stopped in front of her, her body tensed with panic.

'I told you to keep it short and simple. Clearly what I should have said was tell the truth.' His eyes hardened. 'Please don't insult me by trying to pretend you "pressed the wrong button..."'

Daisy felt the walls of the huge office shrink inwards. In his dark suit, his broad shoulders blocking the light, Rollo Fleming dominated the space around them. But she couldn't allow him to dominate *her*. If she did, then the truth would come out and David's life would be ruined.

She tried to let out her breath without his noticing.

'You're not the only one who's had a long day,' she retorted. 'I've been on my feet for hours and I'm tired too. Which is why I made a mistake.'

He shook his head.

'I don't class breaking and entering as a "mistake." And I'll think you'll find most juries agree with me.' His face was hard, anger harshening the fine features. 'So stop prevaricating and tell me why you're sneaking about in my office at quarter to one in the morning.'

'I didn't know it was your office.' She forced herself to meet his face. 'How could I? I don't even know who you are.'

His expression shifted into one of pure disbelief.

'You're working downstairs and you don't know who I am?'

Daisy glowered at him. His derisive tone, coupled with his arrogant and irritatingly correct assumption that she would know who he was, made her see red.

'I work for lots of people,' she said stubbornly. 'I don't remember all their names and faces.'

Watching his mouth tighten, she felt a stab of satisfaction at having punctured his pride.

There was a long, abrasive silence and then he shrugged. 'Which is no doubt why you're just a waitress.'

Her cheeks flooded with heat, his sneer stinging like a slap.

Just a waitress!

'Don't patronise me—' she began furiously.

'Then don't lie to me,' he said softly.

She glared past him, face flushed. 'Fine. So I

know who you are! So what? It makes no difference to me—'

'Then you are either exceptionally foolish or dangerously foolhardy, because this is *my* building,
and *my* office. *And you shouldn't be in it.*'

His voice scraped against her skin, sending flick-
ers of fear in every direction.

Watching her face turn pale, Rollo felt his stomach twist.

Beneath her bravado she was scared—maybe she
wasn't the hardened criminal he'd taken her to be.

But she *was* still guilty.

Guilty of knowing the power of her beauty and
guilty of exploiting it to deceive and disarm. He
stared at her critically, noting the slight tilt of her
chin, the wash of colour on the flawless cheekbones. He'd known women like her before. One in
particular, who had thought nothing of lying and
manipulating those around her, causing havoc and
devastation even as she played the victim.

Daisy had made the biggest mistake of her life if
she thought her charms would work on him and,
eyes narrowing, he let the silence lengthen until
finally, with a mixture of defiance and almost ex-

aggerated casualness, she said, 'I was curious. I just wanted to have a look around.'

'I see.' He loaded his words with sarcasm. 'And yet you didn't put on the lights? You must have truly extraordinary night vision.'

Daisy bit her tongue. Already she hated that sneer, the way his eyebrows lifted, and the glitter in that mocking green gaze. Of course, she'd imagined what would happen if she got caught. But in her head she had pictured some bumbling security guard. She certainly hadn't expected to be grilled by Rollo Fleming himself. The watch's owner and a man who was demanding an honesty she couldn't give.

'I didn't put the lights on because I thought somebody would see,' she said quickly.

He was standing too close; the heat and scent of his body was messing with her head so that speaking in sentences was suddenly a struggle.

'I know this floor is off limits, but I've worked here a couple of times and I wanted to see...'

She paused. *What could she have possibly—believably—wanted to see in an unlit office?*

Blood pounding in her ears, she stared desperately past him at the lit-up skyscrapers—and then her gaze locked on to the Empire State Building.

'The city. At night,' she said, her breath judder-ing in relief. 'Everyone says the view from up here is amazing, so I thought I'd come and look.'

He stared at her for so long and so hard that she had to clench the muscles in her legs to stop them from giving way.

'How?'

She blinked. 'What?'

'Not *what*. *How?* How did you get up to this level? Catering staff only have clearance for the floor they're working on.'

Daisy swallowed. *Keep it simple*, she told her-self. 'I don't know,' she lied again. 'I just pressed some buttons.'

Her head was starting to ache, and there was no way she could keep this up for much longer. It was time for a dignified retreat. David would understand, and together they could think of an-other less humiliating way to return Rollo Flem-ing's watch to him.

She breathed out, fighting for calm. 'Look, Mr Fleming, I'm really sorry I came up here, okay? It was a bad idea—a mistake—and I promise I will never do anything like it again. So if you could just forget I was ever here, I'd be really grateful.'

There was a taut silence as his gaze held hers.

'Daisy. Pretty name…' he said quietly.

She could sense he was battling to control his temper.

'Old-fashioned. Sweet. Decent.'

He smiled—a chilling smile that sent a shiver down her backbone.

'It's a pity you don't live up to it.'

She felt her body still. 'I don't know what you mean,' she said carefully.

He shook his head. 'Then let me explain. I've had a long day…'

Pausing, he felt his shoulders stiffen. Not just long. It had been a day of frustration and failure. The deal was generous—he'd offered way more than the market value of the building—and yet once again James Dunmore had rejected it out of hand. And he still didn't really understand why.

His lips pressed together. Or rather he *did* understand; he just didn't know what to do about it. Dunmore didn't approve of him, or his reputation for ruthlessness and womanising and so he wouldn't sell. Rollo breathed out slowly. But he *wanted* that building—had wanted it for seventeen years—and he wasn't about to give up now.

If only he could somehow persuade Dunmore that he'd changed…

He felt his pulse quicken. It made him feel tense, thwarted, just thinking about it. And now, as if he didn't have enough to deal with, this woman, Daisy, was trying to hustle him.

So call Security, he told himself irritably.

There was no reason for *him* to deal with this.

But, looking up at Daisy, he felt his body twitch.

Except there was.

A beautiful, brown-eyed reason, with a body that made that completely uninspiring uniform look both chic and sexy. His eyes rested on her face. Aside from a faint smudge of pink on her lips, she was make-up-free. But then beauty like hers needed no enhancement. Everything from the soft curves of her mouth to the huge espresso-coloured eyes was designed to seduce.

She had attempted to pull her long blonde hair into some kind of low ponytail, but it was coming loose, and to his annoyance he found himself wanting to loosen it more. Could almost imagine what it would feel like between his fingers, the weight of it in his hands, and how it would fall forward when they kissed, the silken strands brushing his face—

Abruptly he lifted his head, his eyes glinting.

'As I was saying, I've had a long, difficult day—'

'Then why don't I just get out of your way?' Heart lurching like a ship at sea, Daisy edged backwards. 'I probably should get back to work anyhow.'

She glanced past him, every fibre in her body focused on reaching the door and freedom, and then her stomach lurched too as he shook his head slowly,

'I don't think so.'

His hand coiled around her wrist, his touch searing her skin. 'You're not going anywhere until you tell me the truth.'

'Let go of me.' She tugged her arm, trying not to give in to the cold, slippery panic curling around her heart like an eel. 'I *have* told you the truth!'

'Enough!'

His voice was sharp and final, like a guillotine falling, and she felt his grip tighten.

'You have done nothing but lie since you opened your mouth. Now, most men might fall for this eyelash-fluttering, little-girl-lost routine, but I'm not most men. So save your pouting and tell me what you're doing here.'

'I'm not pouting.' She jerked her arm free. Stuffing her hands back into her apron, she tightened her fingers involuntarily around the swipe card.

'And most men—most reasonable, decent men— wouldn't be interrogating me about an honest mistake.'

He laughed without humour. 'Honest? I doubt you know the meaning of the word.'

Her hands curled into fists. 'Just because you're some big shot property tycoon, it doesn't give you the right to play judge, jury and executioner. I'm not on trial here.'

'No. But you will be.' He stared at her speculatively. 'At a rough guess facing charges of trespass, unlawful entry, intent to rob—'

'*I* didn't come here to rob anyone,' Daisy snapped. 'If you must know, I came here to—'

Breaking off, she stared at him in horror. Around her the tension in the room had soared, so that suddenly she felt as though the walls and the windows might implode.

His gaze was fixed and unblinking. 'To what?'

She stared at him mutely, frozen, horrified by how close she'd come to betraying David—and then in the beat of her heart she darted past him. But he was too quick, and before her brain had even registered him moving, his arm was curving around her waist and pulling her against the hard muscles of his chest.

It was like an electric shock. For a moment she forgot everything. Everything except the fierce, prickling heat surging through her body, warming her blood and melting her bones, so that in another second she knew her legs would buckle beneath her.

'Let go of me.' Angry, outraged—more by her body's inappropriate response than his restricting grip—she started to punch his arm, but he simply ignored the blows, jerking her closer.

'Stop it,' he said coldly. 'You're not helping yourself.'

'You're hurting me.'

'Then stop fighting me.'

His arm curled tighter, so that his stomach was pressing against her spine. But despite his anger, and even though she could feel his strength, she was surprised to find she wasn't afraid of him physically.

Only there was no time to ponder why that should be the case as he said sharply, 'What's in your hand?'

Instantly all her efforts were concentrated on clenching her fist as tightly as possible. But it was a short, unequal fight, and she watched helplessly as, uncurling her fingers, he prised the security card from her hand.

'Thank you,' he said softly, and abruptly he loosened his grip and jerked her round to face him.

She gazed at him dazedly. Her pulse was racing, her blood thundering like an incoming tide. She felt her stomach tighten painfully as his eyes flickered over the card.

'Where did you get this?'

For a moment she considered telling him the truth. But one look at his face was all it took to convince her that that course of action would not only be foolish but hazardous. He was furious. Beyond furious. He was enraged.

'It was on the floor.'

'Of course it was!'

The jeer in his voice sliced through her skin like a knife, so that she had to swallow against the pain. The air was thickening around her and she was finding it hard to breathe. His anger was overwhelming her. She couldn't fight the way he did—didn't have that desire to win whatever the consequences. Whatever the cost…

'I…I… It must… Someone must have dropped it.'

Rollo shook his head dismissively.

He could deal with her lies. He could even understand why she was lying. But he couldn't deal with all the other lies that were crowding into his head. Lies from the past. Conversations between his parents. His mother darting between stories, swapping truths—

Suddenly he just wanted it over. Wanted her out of his office and out of his life.

Lip curling, he glanced to where she stood, wide-eyed, the pulse in her throat jerking unevenly.

'I know this looks bad,' she said haltingly. 'But I wasn't doing anything wrong. You have to believe me—'

'I think we both know it's a little late for that,' he said savagely.

He didn't trust her, and for good reason. Life had taught him at an early age that there was nothing more disingenuous or dangerous than a cornered woman.

But this one wasn't his problem.

'I'm tired,' he said bluntly. 'And this conversation is over.'

He reached into his jacket and pulled out his phone.

'What do you mean? Who are you calling? No. Please—'

He felt his stomach soar upwards, snagged by the desperation in her voice even as anger swept over him like lava. Was she really going to keep this up? This pretence that she'd come up here to see the view.

'I gave you a chance to tell the truth. That you came here to steal from me—'

'But I didn't.' Her voice was husky with emotion. 'I admit I lied to you. But I swear I'm not a thief.'

He held her gaze. It would be easy to believe her. She sounded so convincing. But then he remembered how she had fought him for the swipe card, with fire—not fear—in her eyes, and glancing at her face he could see tautness—the nervous dread of a skater standing on thin ice, waiting to hear it crack.

But *why*? What was there left to dread?

His shoulders tensed. And then, as his gaze dropped down to the short black apron, he saw her face freeze. He felt a dizzying anger like vertigo. Slowly he moved in front of her, his powerful body blocking her exit.

'Prove it. Empty out your pockets,' he said tersely. 'Unless you want me to do it for you.'

She shrank away from him, eyes widening with

unmistakable guilt, her face pale with shock and uncertainty. 'Are you threatening me?'

'I don't know,' he said, his voice soft, light, his face sculptured with menace. 'Do you feel threatened?'

Daisy swallowed. Yes. She did. And not just threatened. Trapped. But how could she do what he asked? If he saw the watch—*his watch*—there was zero chance of her getting out of the office, let alone the building.

'I can explain…' But her words faltered as she realised that she couldn't.

Rollo stared at her in silence. A sudden vivid memory of his mother saying exactly the same words slid into his head, and he let them echo and fade until he was able to speak.

'I'm sure you can. But I think I've had enough bedtime stories for one evening.'

His words sent a chill through her.

'Don't worry though. I'm sure someone else will find them far more entertaining.' He paused, a cold smile curling his lips. 'Like my security team. We can go and talk to them right now. They're downstairs with David—your brother. Waiting to take you both to the police station.'

CHAPTER TWO

DAISY STARED AT him in horror. His words were burning inside her head, so hot and bright she couldn't think straight. Finally she forced herself to speak.

'What's David got to do with any of this?'

But even as the question left her lips, she knew there was no point in pretending any more. There was only one possible explanation for why her brother was with Security.

Rollo knew everything.

The thought made her feel dizzy and she took a quick, shallow breath, trying not to give in to the damp chill sweeping over her skin.

'You know about…? That David…?'

'That your brother stole my watch?'

His gaze held hers, the derision in his voice making her cheeks burn.

'I knew the day he stole it. My office has security cameras. Your brother was caught on film.'

He paused and, looking up, she saw the glittering contempt in his eyes, felt her stomach cramp with fear. He'd known right from the start—before she'd even steeled herself to step into the lift. He'd simply been watching, waiting…

Waiting for her to realise that fact.

All her carefully laid plans had been for nothing. Suddenly she was struggling to hold it together.

'Please—'

Her voice sounded all wrong, high and breathless, not at all like her voice. But maybe that was because she was no longer Daisy Maddox but some anonymous criminal. The thought made fear crystallise on her skin like ice.

'Please don't do this. I know it looks bad. But if you'll just give me five minutes—'

His eyes narrowed. 'I think you've wasted more than enough of my time already.'

'But you don't know the full story,' she protested.

'Story? More like fantasy!' He shook his head. 'Save it for your lawyers. They'll be *paid* to listen to your lies. I'm not.'

His derisive words punched through her panic. The man was a monster! Didn't he understand what breaking into his office had cost her?

Suddenly her whole body was rigid and vibrating with anger. 'I might have known someone like you would bring it all back to money,' she snapped.

'Someone like me?' His voice was chillingly cold. 'You mean a law-abiding citizen?'

She glowered at him. 'I mean someone without a heart.'

His eyes glinted threateningly beneath the lights. 'I don't need a heart to recognise a thief.'

'David's not a thief.' Her head jerked up.

'So he didn't steal my watch?'

'No—I mean yes. But it was a mistake—'

'I'm sure the prisons are littered with people all saying the same.'

'No, you don't understand—'

'And I don't want to.' He frowned at her impatiently. 'Your brother's motives are of no interest to me. I'm only concerned with his guilt.' His gaze didn't flicker. 'And yours.'

Daisy stared at him open-mouthed.

'*My* guilt!'

His lip curled up impatiently.

'Look, I may not have a heart, but I do have a brain and I'm not stupid. You didn't come up here by accident, or to look at the view. You came to see what else you could steal—'

'*No.*' Her voice echoed around the empty office. 'I did not.'

'Yes, you did.' The finality in his voice sent a warning chill through her. 'As whatever you've got stashed in those pockets will no doubt demonstrate when we get downstairs.'

She gazed at him dumbly. Something had just hit her. A way to corroborate her story. Desperately she fumbled inside her apron and pulled out the watch.

'I didn't break in here to steal from you,' she said breathlessly. 'I came to bring this back.'

If she'd been expecting flags and a parade, she would have been disappointed. Rollo barely glanced at the watch. Instead his eyes were fixed on her face.

'That proves nothing. Or rather, given that it contradicts everything you've just said, it merely confirms that you're a liar as well as a thief!'

Her hands were trembling. She felt almost giddy with anger. 'I'm not a thief.'

He shrugged. 'Unlike some people, I prefer to tell *and* hear the truth.'

'In that case you're a bully.'

'Is that right?' His shoulders rose and tensed.

'Yes, it is. Ever since you walked through that

door you've done nothing but make threats and try to intimidate me.'

A muscle flickered in his cheek, and then slowly he held out his phone.

'So call the police,' he said softly. 'Go on. Call them.'

Her pulse gave a jerk. She had effectively backed herself into a corner, and he knew it. But watching his green eyes gleam triumphantly, his smug assumption that she would back down, flipped a switch inside her head. Stepping forward, she snatched the phone from his hand.

'Fine. I will,' she snarled. 'At least that way I won't have to spend any more time with you.'

'Don't be so bloody childish.'

There was a tension in his voice she hadn't heard before.

'I'm not being childish,' she snapped. 'You're going to call them anyhow, so what does it matter?'

Their eyes locked—hers furiously defiant, his cool, opaque, dispassionate—and then her mouth curved scornfully.

'Oh, I get it. *You* wanted to do it. So who's being childish now?'

There was a small, tight silence.

Rollo took a slow, deep breath. His chest felt hot

and taut. Her stubbornness was infuriating, and yet part of him couldn't help admiring her. She was just so determined to keep fighting him—even to the point of making this crazy kamikaze gesture.

Glancing from her face to her tightly curled hands, he sighed. 'You don't want to do that, Daisy,' he said at last.

'You don't know *what* I want. You don't know anything about me or David.'

He met her gaze. 'So tell me.'

Daisy stared at him in silence. Why was he offering her a chance to talk now? More than anything she wanted to hurl it back in his face. But already her anger was fading and picturing her brother waiting, wordless with terror downstairs, she took a shallow breath and lowered the phone.

'Why?' she said sulkily. 'So you can use it against him.'

His eyes narrowed. 'That depends on what you tell me. To date, all I know about your brother—aside from his penchant for expensive watches—is that he works in Acquisition and Development. And he's tall and twitchy—'

'He's not twitchy. He's just a bit nervous.' She spoke defensively and instantly wished she hadn't as he turned his penetrating, unsettling green gaze on her face.

'Guilty people often are.'

There was no short or easy way to refute that statement, so instead she satisfied herself with giving him an icy glare.

'He's not some criminal mastermind. He's shy, and he finds it difficult to make friends with people.'

'He might find it easier if he didn't steal from them,' he said smoothly.

'It was a mistake.' Her voice rose with exasperation.

'So you keep saying. But a mistake is when you forget to charge your phone. Not when you purposely steal something that doesn't belong to you. That's called theft.'

'Not always.' She looked him straight in the eye, her shoulders set high and pushed back as though for battle. 'Sometimes it's called "charging market rent."'

Rollo gritted his teeth. Not in response to her confrontational remark but because he knew that this time she was telling the truth. David Maddox was clearly not a criminal mastermind. Which was why he'd requested a background check instead of just firing him.

It had taken less than half a day for a file to land on his desk, and the research had been thorough—health records, academic results and employment history. And one line noting the existence of a twin sister who also happened to work for the Fleming Organisation's hospitality team.

Glancing across at her face, he felt his breath suddenly light and loose in his chest; he felt weightless, off balance, as though he'd been drinking. That was all she'd been. A line in a report. A name without a face.

But no words could ever have conveyed Daisy's beauty and spirit. Or the way her eyes softened when she talked about her brother. Or that tiny crease she got on her forehead when she was digging in her heels.

His fingers twitched and suddenly, more than anything, he wanted to reach out and touch the curve of her cheek, then carry on touching, his fingers sliding over the soft skin of her throat, then lower still, to the swelling curves of her breasts and waist—

He felt his body jerk to life—muscles tightening, groin hardening.

Sitting watching the camera footage of her breaking into his office, he'd thought she was beautiful but greedy—a woman who didn't believe the rules applied to her. And it had angered him so much that for reasons he didn't want to examine, he'd broken with protocol and convinced his security team to let him deal with her personally.

Only now here she was, clutching his phone like an amulet to ward off evil, and he couldn't seem to hold on to his anger. At least not the vindictive, punitive kind. Instead—and he really couldn't explain why—he felt wound up, and almost irritated by her reckless stupidity.

Had she really thought she could get away with it?

Then she was not only foolhardy but utterly deluded; there was no way he would ever have fallen for her lies.

Except that he would have done.

His muscles tensed as the truth hit him square in the chest: if he hadn't watched her breaking in he would have believed every word, trusted each hesitant glance. She would have had him eating out of her hand.

The thought should have repelled him, but instead he felt his pulse accelerate, the blood humming inside his head, as slowly, miraculously he realised that maybe—just maybe—he had found a way to change James Dunmore's mind.

Gazing blandly over at her, he shrugged. 'Obviously I'd love to hear your views on social housing some other time, but right now I think we should talk about *you.*'

There was a startled pause. She stared at him suspiciously. 'Why?'

He shrugged. 'I'm curious. What do you do when you're not breaking into offices?' he said softly.

'Why do you care?' she snapped. 'You've clearly made up your mind that David and I are some of kind of Bonnie and Clyde. Nothing I say is going to change that.'

'Try me,' he said lazily. 'I can't say for sure that it'll change anything. But what have you got to lose?'

Holding her breath, Daisy watched in mute fascination as he reached up and undid the top button of his shirt, tugging the dark green tie loose to reveal a triangle of sleek golden skin.

Angry, Rollo Fleming was formidable, but she was just starting to realise that anger was not the most effective weapon in his armoury. His charm was far more lethal. And when the chill and distance left his voice he was at his most dangerous.

'You said earlier you weren't interested,' she said stiffly.

'And you said earlier I didn't have a heart.'

His gaze rested on her face—cool, unblinking, unreadable—and her own heart skipped a beat.

'So what are you saying?'

'I'm giving you an opportunity to redeem yourself. And David, of course.'

Rollo could see she was tempted by his words. He could read the conflict in her eyes, her distrust of him battling with her impulse to protect her brother. He waited, knowing the value of both silence and patience, until finally she sighed.

'There's not much to say. I'm twenty-five. I live with my brother, who's my twin. And I'm a waitress.' Her eyes flared. *'Just a waitress.* But not through choice. I'm actually an actress, only I'm between jobs at the moment.'

There was a sharp, complicated silence.

'That's it.' She looked up defensively. 'I told you there wasn't much.'

Rollo studied her in silence. There was a flush of colour on her cheeks and her eyes were daring him to prove her right.

'Depends on your definition of "much",' he said smoothly. 'A half-point swing in my commodities portfolio could cost me millions of dollars.'

Daisy stared at him warily. Something was happening around her, silent and unseen.

She narrowed her eyes. 'What do you want?'

The corners of his mouth curved upwards into a tiny satisfied smile.

'Let's just say that I think I've found a way for all of us to move on from this unfortunate incident.'

A fresh fear rose up inside her. 'I'm not going to have sex with you, if that's what you mean. I'd rather sell my kidneys!'

'I believe the norm is only one.' He stared at her impassively, his green gaze colder and harder than any emerald. 'And don't flatter yourself, Ms Maddox. I like a woman in handcuffs as much as the next man, but not when the only reason she's wearing them is because she's been arrested.'

She bit her tongue. 'So what *do* you want, then?'

He scrutinised her for a long moment, almost as though he were trying to see through her or past her. It made her feel taut, trapped—vulnerable, a deer gazing into the headlights of an oncoming car.

Finally he smiled—a smile that tore the breath out of her.

'I want you to be my wife,' he said softly.

There was a moment of pure, absolute silence.

She gazed at him in shock, trying to catch up. The last few hours had proved unequivocally that Rollo was a cold-blooded megalomaniac, but now it appeared he was also utterly and irrefutably insane.

'I'm sorry.' She shook her head slowly. 'I think I must have misheard you. I thought you said—'

'That I want you to be my wife.' His eyes flickered over her stunned expression. 'You heard correctly.'

Breathing out unsteadily, she lifted her hand to her forehead, as though to ward off the insanity of his suggestion.

'What are you talking about?' she managed.

It must be some kind of trick or trap—another way to make her look stupid and feel small. She stared wildly round the room, hoping to find some explanation. But turning back to meet his gaze she felt a shudder of alarm ripple over her skin.

He was being serious!

She stared at him incredulously.

'You barely know me. And we hate each other. Why would you want to marry me?'

He paid no attention. 'Why don't you sit down and we can talk about it properly?'

He was just like a politician, she thought desperately. Answering a question with a question. Ignoring what he couldn't answer or didn't want to discuss.

She opened her mouth to protest but he was already walking past her, and as she watched him take a seat behind the huge glass-topped desk she felt her ribs expand. He looked calm, relaxed, as though he often proposed marriage to young women who broke into his office in the early hours of the morning. But his eyes were alert and predatory, like a wolf watching a lamb stumble around in its lair.

'Come on. Sit down. I don't bite.'

It wasn't an invitation. It wasn't even an order. It was a dare.

She lifted her chin.

'Fine. But I can't see what difference talking will make. Nobody marries a complete stranger.'

Sinking into the soft leather, she felt the tiredness of the last few hours rise up beneath her skin in a wave as, lounging back in his seat, he stared past her, in a way that suggested he was pondering some deep philosophical question.

'Is that true? Plenty of brides all over the world only meet their husband on their wedding days.'

'Yes. If they're having an arranged marriage.' She glowered at him.

'But we are.' He smiled a smile that made her wish that his chair would open up and swallow him whole. 'And *I'm* arranging it.'

Daisy felt her skin grow warm; her head was spinning. 'Don't be ridiculous. You're not arranging anything,' she snapped. 'Look, you can't want to marry me, so why are you pretending you do?' She stared at him doubtfully. 'Is it your idea of a joke? Some way to punish me for…?'

Looking up at him, she felt her words falter in her mouth. For an endless moment he studied her in silence and then, leaning forward, he fixed his eyes on hers with an intentness that seared her skin.

'If I wanted to punish you, I'd think of something a lot more…*diverting.*'

Her stomach clenched, and a tingling excitement swept through her like fire through a forest as he smiled slowly.

'For both of us.'

A hot shiver ran up her spine and she stared at him mutely, her body stilling even as chaos raged inside. Her heart was beating too fast and too loud, and a dark ache was swirling over her skin like a riptide. In an effort to break the spell of his gaze, she pressed her nails hard into the palms of her hands.

'You can't just tell someone you're marrying them,' she said carefully. 'It doesn't work like that.'

The tension in the room quivered, as though she had somehow pressed her foot onto an accelerator pedal, and her eyes flickered involuntarily across to where Rollo sat, examining her with detached curiosity.

'It does if you want your brother to keep his job. And, more important, to stay out of prison.'

She was out of her seat and leaning across his desk before she had even realised she was moving, her whole body shaking with shock and anger.

'You unspeakable pig!' Her voice rose. 'That's blackmail—'

'Yes, it is.'

He wasn't even embarrassed! Furiously, she glanced around for something blunt and heavy.

'Why are you getting so bent out of shape about this?' He stared at her calmly.

'Why? *Why?* Maybe because it's weird and wrong.' Heat was blistering her skin. She couldn't keep the shake out of her voice. 'You're cynically exploiting this situation for your own ends.'

He frowned. 'You're being melodramatic. You and I marrying will be mutually beneficial. As to the morality of blackmailing a thief and a liar, I'm not sure we have time to tackle that right now, so why don't you just calm down and sit down?'

He lifted his arms behind his head and stretched out his shoulders.

'Sit down,' he said again, and this time there was no mistaking the authority in his voice. 'I didn't explain myself properly. I need to marry you, but in essence you'll just be playing the part of my wife.'

She felt a rush of hope. 'You mean like in an advert or something? For your business?' He stared at her in silence.

'No. Not like an advert. We're going to have to marry legally.'

Daisy searched his face, looking for answers, for a way to escape the certainty in his voice. 'Why can't we just pretend?'

He shook his head slowly. 'That won't work. It can't just *look* like we're married. It has to be legal.'

'But no one needs a wife that badly,' she said almost viciously. 'Not at two o'clock in the morning.'

He shrugged. 'I do.'

'But why?'

'That doesn't concern you.' The certainty in his voice had hardened to granite.

She stared at him, sensing that somewhere a door was closing, a key was turning. Soon there would be no way out of this mess.

She felt her temper flare. 'Fine. But I'm not marrying anyone—especially you—unless you tell me why you need a wife.'

It wasn't just curiosity. She needed to assert herself. Needed him to know that she wasn't just some puppet on a string.

She folded her arms in front of her chest. 'I don't need details. Just keep it short and simple.'

She held her breath as his eyes narrowed into knifepoints, and she knew he was gauging how much he needed to tell her. Finally he shrugged and met her gaze, cool and back in control again.

'I'm trying to close a deal. For a building I want to buy. The owner is old-fashioned…sentimental. He'll only sell to someone he trusts. Someone he believes shares his values. I need him to trust me and for that to happen he needs to see my warmer, softer side. Marriage is the simplest way to demonstrate that to him.'

She breathed out slowly. There was a kind of warped logic to his argument.

'But surely I can't be your only solution? What if you hadn't found me in your office? What would you do then?'

His eyes were watching hers. 'But I did find you. And you're perfect.'

Her heart thudded against her ribs and she felt her cheeks grow warm. 'I—I am?'

Rollo felt his groin grow hard, his body responding not only to her tentative question but to the flush of colour in her cheeks, the pulse jerking at the base of her throat. She was like a flint striking, sparking against him, catching fire.

And fire burned.

Ignoring the twitch of lust in his groin, he breathed out slowly. 'Yes. You're single. And you're an actress. But primarily, and most important, I can trust you to be compliant.'

Daisy knew she had gone white.

'Compliant?' Her hands were trembling.

'Out-of-work actresses are ten a penny. But I need someone I can depend on. And as your brother's freedom and future are in my hands I'm confident I can rely completely on your discretion.'

He sounded so calm and controlled that she thought she might throw up. Was this how people got to the top in business? By turning every situation to their advantage no matter what the collateral damage?

'But, of course, if you'd rather take your chances with the police...'

He let his sentence drift off as Daisy stared past him. She felt bruised, battered and beaten.

'How long would it be for?' she said dully.

'A year. Then we'd go our separate ways and the slate would be wiped clean.'

She flinched inside. He made it sound so simple. The perfectly packaged, one-use-only relationship. An entirely disposable marriage. And maybe it was that simple for him, for clearly his brain worked in an entirely different way from hers.

Her heart contracted. But it was so different from the marriage she'd always imagined. Given her failed romantic history, she knew she was more likely to win a starring role on Broadway, but what she wanted was a relationship based on love and trust and honesty. Just like her parents'.

Only that was the polar opposite of what she

and Rollo would have if she agreed to this stupid fake marriage.

The thought made her feel utterly alone.

Pushing back her shoulders, she lifted her head, a flare of defiance sparking inside her. 'And you're okay with that?' she asked flatly. 'It's how you always imagined your marriage?'

Leaning back, Rollo swivelled his chair to face the window. He knew that her question was more or less rhetorical. But the blood was beating in his veins with swift, hot, unreasonable fury.

For a moment he gazed out across the city, silently battling the sickening panic and feeling of helplessness stirred up by their conversation. The short, expurgated answer was *no*—it wasn't the way he'd imagined his marriage. Not because it would be fake and devoid of feeling, but because he had never once imagined being married at all.

Why would he? He knew for a fact that people weren't capable of being satisfied with just one partner. And he certainly didn't believe marriage represented love or devotion.

His mother's behaviour had proved that to him over and over again, slowly destroying their family and his father in the process.

But marriage to Daisy would be altogether different, he reassured himself. It would be carefully controlled *by him* and there would be no risk of pain or humiliation, for that would require an emotional dependency that would be absent from their relationship. In fact, their lives need only really intertwine in public.

Feeling calmer, he turned to face her.

'I can't say I've expended much mental energy on the matter. Personally, I've never seen the point of making such an emotionally charged and unrealistic commitment to somebody.'

Daisy glared at him. 'How romantic! Do you say that to *all* the women you date or just the ones you blackmail?'

He stared at her impassively, but his eyes had darkened in a way that made the breath jam in her throat.

'I never promise anything to anyone I date,' he said, his eyes lingering on her face. 'But you don't need to worry on their account. They want what I want. They're independent women who enjoy having sex. *With me.* And I can assure you they're perfectly satisfied with the arrangement.'

Daisy caught her breath.

'I'll just have to take your word for that,' she said tautly. 'And, just so we're clear, if I do become your wife, I'll play my part in public but our relationship will not extend to the bedroom. You can *satisfy* yourself in private.'

Watching the hard flare of anger in his eyes, she felt a sudden spasm of hope. Rollo might have arrogantly assumed he could conjure up a marriage between two strangers—strangers who despised one another—but clearly he hadn't thought everything through.

So maybe it still wasn't too late to change his mind.

Folding her arms in front of her chest, she tried to replicate the cool, flat expression that was back in place on his face.

'Look, I know you don't want to hear this, but are you really sure we can pull this off? Think about it. We're complete strangers. And we're never going to have sex. So just how are we going to fool everyone into thinking we're some loved-up couple who can't keep their hands off one another?'

She felt her stomach twist. It was a perfect description of her dream relationship. The one she had tried so hard—and failed—to create with each and every one of her boyfriends.

'I don't think that'll be a problem.'

His words bumped into her thoughts and her

pulse jerked as abruptly he got to his feet, his body disturbingly, powerfully muscular and male in the confines of his office.

'Then I think you're being really naive,' she said with more confidence than she felt as he walked slowly around the desk towards her. 'I could probably pull it off. In public at least. But I'm a trained actress. What you're asking is not as easy as it looks. Think of all those films that bomb at the box office because the two leads don't have any chemistry—'

She broke off as he stopped in front of her and held out his hand.

'We need to leave,' he said quietly. 'The security teams will be changing shift soon, and I think we've both answered enough awkward questions already tonight.'

Ignoring his hand, she stood up—but instantly she regretted it, for suddenly they were facing one another, only inches apart. Gazing up at him, she felt her skin grow tight and hot.

'What were we talking about?' he said softly. 'Oh, yes. Our chemistry.'

'It's just not there,' she said hastily, trying not to breathe in the clean, masculine smell of his body.

'And, believe me, you can't just manufacture it for the cameras. It has to be real.'

Rollo let a silence build between them. He wondered if she realised that her body was contradicting her words. That her cheeks were flushed, her lips parted invitingly.

Scrutinising her face, he frowned. 'Well, this thing won't work unless we can convince people.' His eyes narrowed. 'I wonder... How would we test it? If this was a *real* acting job, I mean.'

Her eyes froze midblink. 'I suppose we'd do an audition.'

Taking a step closer, he smiled a small, dispassionate smile. 'What a good idea...' he murmured.

And slowly he lowered his head and kissed her on the lips.

For a fraction of a second he felt her tense against him, and then her mouth softened under his and she was kissing him back...

Daisy curled her fingers into the fabric of his shirt. She knew she should be repelled by his touch. He was her enemy, a bully and a blackmailer. But instead she felt her body catch fire as he deepened the kiss, his mouth suddenly fierce against hers.

A shock—sharp, raw and electric—ran over her

skin and her body jerked against his, her hands coming up to grip his arms, her nails cutting into the muscle. She felt him respond, heard the quickening of his breath, felt her own breath stalling in her throat as he arched her body, tipping her head up to meet his—

And then suddenly he lifted his mouth and breathed out softly.

'What was it you said? Oh, that's right. It has to be *real*.' His lips curved upwards and he stroked a strand of hair away from her face. 'I'd say that was pretty damn real.'

There was no mistaking the gleam of satisfaction in his eyes.

Daisy stared at him dazedly. Her heart was slamming into her ribcage. With shock and more than a little embarrassment she realised that her fingers were still wrapped around his arm and slowly, cautiously, not wanting to draw attention to the fact, she lifted her hand.

He watched her calmly. 'So... Last chance. What's it to be? Me? Or the police?'

Daisy flinched. The bluntness of his question was like a punch to the jaw. If it had been just her, she wouldn't have hesitated. She would have turned him down right there and then. He was ruthless and cold-blooded. The relationship he was suggesting would be a travesty of everything she believed. Why, then, was she considering marrying a man she hated with whom she would share nothing but a lie?

Because it wasn't just about her. There were other people to consider. Not just David but her parents too.

Before she could change her mind, she met his gaze and said quickly, 'You.'

He smiled a small triumphant smile that made panic trickle over her skin, cold and damp like rain. She was too ashamed of herself to care. Too ashamed that her decision had been made not solely out of love and loyalty but because being with Rollo would mean that, just for a while, she could forget Daisy Maddox and her hopeless dreams of true love. Because right now finding the right man was a whole lot scarier than the thought of faking it with the wrong one.

'Good. Then we should leave.'

'I want to see David—'

He shook his head. 'Another time. He needs to go home.' His eyes met hers—clear, green, assessing. 'And you need to come with me. To the Upper

East Side,' he said lazily. 'Your home for the next twelve months.'

Home! The word sounded so warm and friendly. Daisy bit her lip. It seemed unlikely, but maybe Rollo really did have a softer, warmer side. And silently she prayed that he did. Otherwise she was going to spend the next twelve months feeling like an inmate at the world's most exclusive prison.

CHAPTER THREE

I AM SO not ready for this, Daisy thought as just over an hour later she followed Rollo into the hallway of his penthouse on Park Avenue.

Everything was moving so fast.

Waiting in the lift, she'd half thought that the whole crazy plan might just dissolve in the face of reality. But Rollo had overseen all the arrangements with a quiet, indisputable authority. David had been escorted home and told to take a few days' leave. Daisy's absence had been explained by a hastily concocted plan involving a last-minute callback for a part at a theatre in Philadelphia.

Within minutes of agreeing to become his wife it felt as though time had sped up exponentially, so that one moment she'd been standing in his office and the next she'd been sitting in a sleek black limousine, moving smoothly through traffic towards the Upper East Side.

She might have started to panic sooner, only she had been so distracted by how it had felt when he'd kissed her that she had barely registered the journey. Instead she had simply sat in silence, replaying the moment when his lips had touched hers.

Gazing up, she felt her heartbeat slow. In his office she had just been grateful that Rollo had not called the police. But now that her panic had gone and she was standing in a hallway roughly the same size as David's entire apartment she felt the same mixture of shock and doubt as an astronaut crash-landing on a strange alien planet.

It didn't feel real. It certainly didn't feel like her life anymore.

In front of her a huge chandelier made of crystal droplets cascaded down like a waterfall into the centre of the marble floor, while on the far side of the hallway a staircase wide enough for a car rose gracefully up to a galleried landing. But what drew her attention most were the three vast contemporary canvases on the walls.

Gazing at the one nearest, she frowned. It looked familiar…

'It's a Pollock. One of his earlier works.'

Her pulse jolted forward like a startled deer. Engrossed by her new surroundings, she had completely forgotten that Rollo was there. But her shock was quickly supplanted as his words registered on her brain.

A Pollock! Rollo owned an actual Jackson Pollock.

The thought blew her mind.

Theoretically, she knew he was rich, but this was a real work of art—the sort that fetched millions at auction. And it was in his hallway.

Hoping she didn't look as gauche as she felt, she nodded nonchalantly. 'David loves his paintings.'

'Personally I find them a little busy. But these...' he gestured casually towards the walls '...weren't my choice anyway. My curator picked them. He thinks they have the greatest potential to rise in value.'

Tearing her eyes away from the paintings, Daisy frowned. 'And that's what matters, is it? That they make you money? Not that they give you pleasure?'

His eyes roamed lazily over her face in a way that made her squirm inside. 'I find they're usually one and the same thing. Shall we go in?'

Staring past him stonily, she took a shallow breath and nodded slowly.

Moments later, she felt her jaw drop as she walked into the open-plan living area.

The room was enormous.

But it wasn't just the size of it that made her eyes widen. It was the opulence oozing from every corner. Glancing sideways, she noticed a beautiful oil painting of a woman gazing dazedly upwards at a colonnaded ruin. She looked mythical, possibly Greek or Roman. Maybe she had just stumbled across the place where the gods lived. If so, Daisy knew exactly how she felt.

'Welcome to your new home,' Rollo said softly. 'I won't give you the guided tour now, but this is obviously the living room and the kitchen is over there. In case you get hungry in the night.'

She could feel him watching her, gauging her reaction, but she barely noticed. Eyes flitting nervously around the room, she was trying to remember exactly why she'd agreed to move in with him.

It had seemed to make sense earlier. Move in, spend some time getting to know one another and then announce their engagement.

But what the hell had she been thinking? She couldn't imagine living in this apartment, let alone living in it with Rollo, pretending to be his wife.

As though reading her thoughts, he shrugged his jacket off and, throwing it carelessly onto a huge cream leather sofa, met her gaze.

'You'll get used to it.'

'Will I?'

She glanced around nervously. Everything was so big and bright. As usual, after the end of a shift, she had changed into her own clothes. But her comfortable jeans and baggy sweatshirt made her feel as though she had shrunk. If she stayed, she might disappear altogether.

'I should imagine so—' he paused, his expression coolly assessing '—if you want to keep your brother out of prison.'

It was like a sudden icy shower.

Instantly her fear and doubt evaporated, replaced by a blinding flash of anger. 'You really are a bastard,' she said shakily. 'Why would you even say that? I've said I'll do this and I will. Just leave David out of it.'

Her muscles were quivering. He'd just blackmailed her into being his wife. That wasn't normal and he knew it. Hell, he'd even admitted it back in his office. So why was he acting as though she was overreacting? As though she was making a big deal out of nothing?

She shook her head.

'I don't understand you. Doesn't this bother you in any way? That we're going to have to lie? And keep on lying to so many people? And not just tell lies but live a lie too?'

He raised his eyebrows in the way that she now knew preceded one of his hateful, mocking remarks.

'You've spent all evening lying to me, Daisy. A few more months won't make that much difference.'

Their eyes clashed. She swallowed hard, feeling trapped, hating him for the way he twisted everything to make her sound like the villain.

'Don't you have *any* compassion?'

'Generally, yes. Specifically for you, no. You brought this upon yourself. You and your brother, that is. Besides, quite frankly, lies or no lies, I find it difficult to believe that living in a triplex apartment in Manhattan is going to be that much of a hardship for you.'

'If you say so,' she said stiffly.

It was clear she was wasting her time. She might be struggling with the decision they had made, but clearly Rollo was immune to the concept of guilt. And she couldn't keep challenging him all night. Not without anger anyway, and her anger was fading, the adrenaline draining away like bathwater, so that she was suddenly too tired to argue.

'Do you mind if I sit down?' Without waiting for a reply she dropped onto the nearest sofa, stifling a yawn. 'Is there anything else? If not, I'd like to have a hot shower and go to bed.'

Bed!

Rollo felt the word tug at his senses like a kite on a string. It was just three little letters…a place to sleep. But spoken by Daisy in that husky voice it seemed to hint at tangled sheets and bodies moving slowly in the half-light.

Glancing over to where she sat, leaning back against the cushions, he felt his body stiffen in immediate painful response. She was looking up at him with those dark espresso-coloured eyes—eyes that somehow managed to look sleepy yet seductive at the same time.

He gritted his teeth. In his office he'd thought she was beautiful, but now, dressed casually, her legs curling against the leather of the sofa, she looked sexier than any woman he'd ever seen.

Maybe it was the curve of her bottom beneath the tight denim, or the glimpse of bare skin where her oversized sweatshirt was slipping off her shoulder.

The bare skin she would soon be soaping upstairs in the shower.

The thought of her standing naked, water dribbling over her body, was so tantalising that he could suddenly hardly breathe and, swallowing hard, he turned to where a faint pinkish glow through the windows indicated that night was turning to day.

Daisy's desirability was undeniable. But this was a once-in-a-lifetime chance to get what he wanted from James Dunmore. He must be careful not to get distracted by her beauty and her sexual allure.

Clearing his throat, he shook his head. 'No. There's nothing. Everything else can wait…' he glanced round '…until morning,' he finished slowly.

Daisy was asleep, lying on her side, one arm curled under her head like a cat. For a moment he watched her in silence, seeing her as though for the first time—a younger, more vulnerable Daisy. Someone who needed protecting.

The thought needled him, lodging beneath his ribs like a thorn. Why wasn't anyone looking out for her? Her family, her brother, her parents? It made him feel angry all over again only in a different way—angry that she was there on his sofa. That somehow she was now his responsibility.

Responsibility. The word snagged in his throat like a fish bone. Feeling responsible hadn't been part of the equation when he'd come up with the idea of marrying Daisy. It made him feel tense, with its implication of commitment, that somehow there was a bond between them.

Frowning, he ran a hand wearily over his jaw, feeling the scrape of stubble against his fingertips. But was it really such a big deal? All business transactions needed a bond to function. And that was all this was. A transaction. All the rest was just tiredness making him paranoid.

Sighing, he leaned forward, picked up his jacket and gently draped it over her shoulder. She shifted in her sleep, murmuring, fingers splaying apart, and he held his breath. But she didn't wake and finally, after one last look, he turned and walked slowly away.

Waking, it took Daisy a moment to realise where she was. Drowsily she twisted over, sensing daylight, wondering why she had forgotten to draw the curtains in her bedroom. And then her eyes snapped open and instantly her body stilled as she remembered exactly where she was. And why.

Heart beating fast, she lay rigid, the breath trapped in her throat, her limbs stiff, until her muscles began to ache and finally she forced herself to sit up. She gazed warily around the huge living room. There was no sign of Rollo, but her relief was tempered with a slight sense of uneasiness for she could still sense his presence.

Glancing down, she instantly realised why. Someone, presumably Rollo, had covered her with his jacket while she was asleep. Tentatively she picked it up, and inhaled the clean citrus scent of his cologne from the fabric.

The thought of his cool green eyes watching her while she slept made her feel edgy, exposed. He was the enemy, and yet he had seen her at her most vulnerable. It was unsettling. Almost as unsettling as the idea that he had tried to make her comfortable. It seemed a strangely caring gesture from a man who was entirely lacking in empathy.

Her phone vibrated inside her pocket and, pulling it out, she forgot all about Rollo. It was a text from David, along with two earlier messages she had missed.

Scrolling down, she read them slowly, a lump swelling in her throat as she realised how completely her brother trusted her. Not only had he believed her explanation for why he was being allowed to keep his job, but he was almost unbearably grateful to Rollo for being so *'understanding, compassionate, forgiving...'*

Remembering her hurried phone call to him from the limo, she sighed. It hadn't been her most convincing performance, only David had been too exhausted and relieved to notice the strain in her voice or question the credibility of her story. But she knew he might not be so easily persuaded the next time so she'd agreed with Rollo that it would be better not to speak to him in person again for a couple of days.

Leaning forward, Daisy tried to ease the sudden thickness in her throat. She loved her brother. Only right now and for the first time ever, she was glad not to have to hear his voice.

Of course, she was relieved and happy that her brother's life was back on track. He would keep his job and with his debt almost cleared, he could put everything behind him. But a small, whining voice inside her head kept on asking the same question.

What about me? What about my life?

Her stomach gave a low, protesting rumble, as though it was objecting to her selfishness, and sliding her phone back into her pocket she took a deep, calming breath.

What was done was done. And what was more

it had been *her* choice, not David's, to go along with Rollo's crazy suggestion. David knew nothing about it and there was no way she was going to tell him either. She knew her brother—he would want her to call the whole thing off or, more likely, she would convince him to let her carry on and the guilt would destroy him.

Far better just to let him think that everything was back to normal. And then, at some unspecified point in the future, she would tell him and her parents, her friends—the whole world, in fact— about her 'relationship' with Rollo. The thought made her breath hitch higher in her throat.

David was her twin. They told one another everything. Lying to him, and about something so personal and important, was going to be difficult—especially when the shock of it was still so new to her.

Her stomach grumbled again more loudly.

But right now, though, there were more pressing matters to address. Like the fact that if she didn't eat soon, she would probably keel over. She needed some food, and then maybe she might take a look around her new 'home.'

And standing up, she went in search of the kitchen.

Later, having eaten, she walked slowly through the apartment, trying to shift the feeling that she was a guest at best, an intruder at worst. Her family's house was large and comfortable, if a little shabby. But with each step here she felt increasingly out of place.

In daylight the apartment was breathtakingly beautiful. Pale wood floors added warmth to the clean white walls and stark, architectural furniture, and huge windows offered striking views of Central Park and the city. The size and the stillness were dazzling, and without Rollo's reaction to consider she simply stood and gazed in speechless silence.

But it was the outdoor space that left her groping for adjectives. Impressive, stunning, jaw-dropping… None did justice to the tile-covered terrace that stretched uninterrupted towards the skyline. Nor could she find a word to capture the impossible luxury of the infinity pool, its mirror-like surface reflecting nothing but sky and the odd passing aeroplane.

And yet, aside from marvelling at the opulence, Daisy found herself oddly unmoved by the apartment. It felt more like a hotel than a home. There were no personal effects to suggest anyone actually *lived* there. Certainly no sign that Rollo was the owner. It could have belonged to anyone. Or no one.

In which case who was she marrying? Daisy thought nervously.

Stepping into yet another stylish room, she stopped in the doorway. There was something different about it. It was still grand. But it had a sense of being 'used' that the other rooms lacked.

Hesitantly, her legs quivering with tension, she walked over to the desk. There was a striking silver bowl on top of the smooth dark wood. Breathing in, she reached out and touched it with a hand that trembled in time to the beating of her heart as, finally, her brain caught up with her feet.

It was an office. Rollo's office.

Now she really *did* feel like she was snooping! Her muscles twitched involuntarily and, despite having only just eaten, she felt a pit open up in the bottom of her stomach.

It was his private space.

'That didn't take long.'

And his voice.

Her fingers jerked back and, muscles tensing, she turned slowly to where Rollo stood watching her, his shoulder pressed against the door frame.

Her heart had stopped beating and for a moment she stared at him in silence, the only sound her breath fluttering in her throat like a moth against a lampshade.

Even in an entire apartment filled with works of art there was nothing that could compete with the flawless symmetry of his face. But it wasn't his face that was making her legs tremble like blancmange. It was the fact that he was wearing a pair of black running shorts.

Just a pair of black running shorts.

Clearly he'd been to the gym; his hair was damp and a towel hung loosely around his neck. Or maybe he always walked around like that, she thought desperately, heat wrapping round her throat and her shoulders like a heavy scarf.

Any ordinary seminaked person would have been unnerved or embarrassed when confronted by someone fully clothed. Rollo, however, seemed not to care. But then why should he? Her gaze roamed furtively over the smooth muscles of his arms and chest. He was gorgeously, unashamedly male and he knew it.

Tearing her eyes away from the hard definition of his taut, golden stomach, and her imagination from what lay beneath the shorts, she looked up at him warily. 'What didn't take long?'

He didn't reply. Instead his dark green gaze fixed on her face as he stepped into the room. His body filled the doorway so that Daisy had a sudden vivid flashback to the night before.

'You didn't. Stealing the family silver and it's only day one.'

His voice was so quiet, the tone so conversational, she might have thought he was joking. But nothing could disguise the cool contempt in his eyes.

'I should warn you the paintings are a lot heavier than they look, even when they're rolled up.'

Breathing in sharply, she felt her cheeks grow cold, then hot. 'I wasn't stealing anything—'

'Of course you weren't. Let me guess.' He interrupted, his mouth curling into a sneer. 'You just wanted to *have a look*?'

Her temper flared. 'Yes. I did. And why shouldn't I? I live here, and at some point in the future I'm going to be your wife. So, yes, I was having a look.' She stared at him pointedly. 'Although, frankly, I think I've seen a lot more than I wanted to.'

There was a sudden strained silence.

'Is that right?'

The sudden harnessed tension in his voice made her stomach shrivel with panic, but she lifted her chin.

'Yes. Yes, it is.'

She wanted it to be true. Wanted to prove that she was immune to him. Wanted to make a dent in that armour-plated arrogance. But almost instantly she regretted her words as, eyes narrowing, he began slowly walking towards her.

She took a hurried step back. 'What are you doing?'

Her eyes widened… Her voice was high and panicky. But he was still moving forward and frantically she held out her hands.

'Stop. Stop it!'

Finally, thankfully, he did so. Only now they were close enough to touch—so close she could feel the heat of his skin. *Too* close, she realised. Too late. With no physical distance between them there was nowhere to hide from that beautiful sculptured body. Or the seductive curving lips. Lips that had kissed her with a fierce, sensual passion she had never experienced before, rendering her both helpless and hungry.

And now that hunger was rising inside her, dark and treacherous as a storm tide, pulling her under.

'Stop what?'

His voice—cool, blade sharp—sliced through her brain.

'All the name-calling, the snide remarks.' Her own voice was shaking and she hated herself for sounding so weak.

Hated her body for responding when it should be rejecting him. But she hated him more for taking over her life. Breathing in sharply, she folded her arms. Only how was anyone going to believe they were in love if there was only hate?

'This is not going to work,' she said as firmly as she could manage. 'Us, I mean. I know in theory it sounded like it could, but—'

Her words vaporised on her lips as his eyes slammed into hers.

'Let me remind you of why you might want to make it work in practice. It's the only way you and your brother are avoiding criminal records.'

Her chest was hard and tight; her throat felt as if it was closing up.

'But I can't live like this for the next twelve months.'

'I don't care.'

She stared at him, her body trembling not with desire now but with anger.

'Oh, I know you don't care!' She glowered at him, furious responses whirling inside her head like sparks from a Catherine wheel. 'You don't care about me or my feelings. You made that clear from the moment we first met—and, yes, I know I was breaking into your office, so you can spare me the part about how I brought it on myself,' she snapped.

His face was hard and impenetrable, like a castle wall, eyes narrowed like arrow slits.

'I'm warning you, Daisy, I've had just about enough of—'

His voice was like a whip crack, but she wasn't going to let him intimidate her.

'Of what? Of me being a human being? With feelings? You can't call me names and—'

'Call you *names*!' He shook his head incredulously.

'Yes. Call. Me. Names.' She punctuated each word clearly and firmly, like Morse code. 'You do it all the time. And it's not fair—'

'Fair?' His face hardened like water turning to ice. 'I've been more than fair. I could have just handed you and your brother over to the police, but I didn't.'

She gave a small strangled laugh. 'That's your

idea of being fair? Blackmailing me to be your wife? You weren't being fair—just self-serving.'

The skin across his cheekbones grew tauter, his eyes glittering like splinters of glass.

'I see it more as a strategic response to a business opportunity.'

His words should hardly have surprised her, let alone upset her—after all she'd agreed to this relationship partly to avoid anything emotional and meaningful. And yet the knowledge that she was just a means to an end still smarted.

'It's a wonder you even have a business if you put this little effort and commitment into all your other deals,' she said stiffly. 'Let me tell you something, *Rollo*, you might not care about me, or my feelings, but you *do* care about this deal. You must, or why else would I be here? But I'm an actress—not a miracle worker. And no one—certainly no one sane and rational—will ever believe our marriage is real if you carry on behaving like this.'

Surely he could understand what she was trying to say. That normal people in a normal relationship needed a level of trust and respect for one another to make it work.

She sighed. 'I know you think it doesn't matter how I feel. That I deserve it even. But it *does* matter because I can't just ignore all the nasty things you say in private and then act all lovey-dovey in public.'

'Why not? Surely that's what acting is.'

His dismissive statement grated over her skin like a serrated knife.

'What, like business is just people signing bits of paper?' She shook her head dismissively, her brown eyes flashing with scorn. 'I'm an actress. So trust me when I say that if you want an audience to believe in your performance, you can't just pretend. You have to believe too. It's not enough just to say you want me to be your wife. You're going to have to *act* a little yourself. And *commit* to the part.'

She exhaled slowly.

'So, even though you don't like me or approve of me, can you just stop sitting in judgement of me and my brother? Otherwise we're not going to be able to pull this off.'

His gaze rested on her face. 'You broke into my office and he stole my watch. Doesn't that give me some right to judge?'

'No. It doesn't,' she said with spirit. 'All you know about David is that he's tall, twitchy and took your watch.' Picturing her brother, she felt her hands start to tremble. 'But you don't know the real David. The David I know. He's never done anything like this, ever. He's the most law-abiding person you'll ever meet. And the sweetest.'

Watching her eyes soften as she defended her brother, Rollo felt a tightness in his chest. There was something about Daisy and her devotion to her brother that touched him. Something he'd consciously chosen never to imagine. Only now it was here—inside his head, inside his home.

And it made him feel jaded and hollow, so that for a moment it was as though they'd traded places and he was the one creeping through a darkened office. Only he was intruding on something far more personal and private than an empty building.

She might not know truth from fiction, but her love for David was real and pure and unassailable.

His shoulders tightened, muscles setting.

Unassailable and undermining.

He clenched his jaw. Forget drugs and alcohol. Love was a far greater threat to health and happiness; it turned perfectly rational people into fools and strength into weakness. Love betrayed those it should protect and protected those who betrayed others.

He knew that from personal experience. His father's total and unswerving love for his mother had been rewarded not with loyalty but defection. Worse, he had watched his mother weep, felt her pain as his own, only to realise that what he'd taken for misery had actually been self-pity and frustration. Only there had been no way of knowing that until it was too late. When all that had been left was a letter on the kitchen table.

It was why he'd sworn never to make the same mistake as his father. And why, when opportunity presented itself, he was choosing to 'marry' Daisy—a woman he didn't and would never love.

Jaw tightening, Rollo stared past her, his guarded expression giving no hint of the turmoil inside his head.

'If he's so law-abiding and sweet, why did he steal my watch?'

Daisy blinked. Her palms were suddenly damp. It was a reasonable question, and she wanted to tell him the truth. Only how much should she tell? The little she knew about Rollo didn't exactly encourage her to expect a sympathetic reaction. But, glancing up at his set, still face, she realised it was a risk she was going to have to take.

'He needed the money. He's been gambling online. And losing. A lot.'

Saying it out loud, she felt shock again. The same stomach-plunging mix of terror and denial she'd felt when David had finally broken down and told her the truth. Remembering the sharpness of his breath, the fluttering panic in his eyes as she'd tried to calm him down, she felt her vision blur and her stomach cramp around a hard, cold lump of misery.

'I think it was fun at first,' she said quietly. 'Something to do when he couldn't sleep. And then suddenly he had this huge, horrible debt.'

She could feel the misery spreading out and over her, like dark clouds blotting out the sun.

'And now?'

She looked up.

'He didn't sell the watch, so is he still in debt?' He was staring at her impassively—watching, waiting—but for the first time since they'd met, she felt he wasn't judging her.

'I paid most of it off with my savings,' she admitted. 'I did a few commercials last summer. They're not really acting, but they pay well.'

He nodded. 'And has he spoken to anyone about his problem? Other than you, I mean. Friends, maybe? Your parents?'

She shook her head. How could she explain

about her parents? About their marriage, their life together. About how it was what *she* wanted to have. Maybe not their diner, the Love Shack—she'd had enough waitressing to last her a life-time—but they were so supportive and happy. She and David would never do anything to jeopardise that happiness.

'He didn't—we don't want them to know. They'd only worry. Besides…' she added, meeting his gaze '…I—we can sort it out.'

Rollo studied her face. Wrong, he thought si-lently. This kind of problem could never be sorted out without professional help. Addicts rarely be-lieved that they had a problem, no matter what pain and chaos they caused to those around them. And sometimes even when they did, it made little if any difference to their behaviour.

'So when did he tell you?' he said at last. 'About the gambling.'

She swallowed. 'The same day he stole your watch.'

He was silent a moment, considering her an-swer. Then he said quietly, 'Selfish of him, don't you think?'

Her head jerked up. But what had she expected?

Had she really believed Rollo would understand? Or care.

Rollo Fleming.

A man who thought nothing of exploiting another man's moment of weakness or a woman's affection for her brother. She felt sick, her stomach lurching. She had betrayed her brother's confidence, and for nothing.

She glared at him. 'He's not selfish—' she began. But he cut in.

'He's your twin. He must have known that you'd step up and sort it out for him.'

He held up his hand as she started to protest.

'I'm not judging him, Daisy. But addicts don't think like other people. They lie and deny and prevaricate and make excuses. It's part of their sickness.'

She watched his face carefully. It sounded as if he knew what he was talking about and she wanted to ask him how. Or maybe who. But his expression was distant, discouraging, as though he knew that she was trying to figure out the meaning behind his remark.

She nodded mutely.

He met her gaze. 'David is sick. He needs care and support.'

His eyes were cool and untroubled, but his expression had shifted into something she hadn't expected to see; it was oddly gentle...almost like sympathy.

'Which is why I'm going to arrange for him to receive professional help at a clinic.'

Daisy's heart stopped. Unsteadily she pushed back her hair, trying to make sense of his words. 'Why?' she said finally. 'Why would you do that?'

Why, indeed?

Rollo gazed at her taut face. The fine cheekbones and delicate jaw were offset perfectly by her pale, almost-luminous skin. She was very beautiful. But that wasn't the reason he was going to help her brother.

He didn't approve of what David had done. Theft was still theft. Nor did he agree with how Daisy had behaved. But he understood their motives better now.

He shrugged. 'Despite what you think, Daisy, I'm not a complete monster. He needs treatment. As his employer, I feel some responsibility for his welfare. But there is one condition.'

His voice was quiet but she heard the warning note—felt it echo inside her and through her head to the corners of the room.

'I'll take care of David but I won't be messed around. You might not be on my payroll, but you work for me now, and I expect…' He paused, his eyes pulling her gaze upwards like a tractor's headlight beam. 'I demand honesty from my staff.'

Forcing herself to meet his eyes, she gave him a small, tight smile. 'I understand. And thank you for helping David. It's very kind of you.'

He nodded. 'Leave it with me.'

Pulling out his phone, he glanced at the screen and frowned.

'Right. I'm going to go and change.' He paused again. 'Which reminds me—you need to go shopping.'

The change of subject caught her off guard.

'I do?'

His gaze held hers. 'There's a charity fashion show a week from tomorrow. I think it should be our first public appearance. We'll be ready by then.'

Daisy flinched inwardly. He wasn't asking, but telling her, and his cool statement was yet another reminder of the fact that she was dealing with a man who always got what he wanted, one way or another.

He stared at her calmly. 'It won't be too formal or

intimate, and you'll be visible but anonymous, so it will be the perfect moment to introduce you as my girlfriend. But you'll need something to wear. Kenny, my driver, knows which stores to go to. Just choose whatever you like and charge it to my accounts.'

'That's very generous.' She frowned. 'But I don't expect you to buy my clothes. Besides, I have quite a few back at David's,' she said, trying to make a joke.

But he didn't laugh. Instead he stared at her, for so long and so intently that she wasn't sure if he'd actually heard her. But then, finally, he smiled coldly.

'I'm sure your clothing was adequate for your life before, but trust me—you'll feel more comfortable in something a little more *appropriate*.'

Adequate! Appropriate!

Hands curling into fists, Daisy gazed at him in angry disbelief.

Moments earlier she had felt…if not close to Rollo, then at least more relaxed with him. Now though, she was remembering just how much she loathed him.

He was so unspeakably arrogant and autocratic.

'Shouldn't it be up to *me* to decide what is appropriate?' she said tightly.

'Ordinarily, yes. But that was before you agreed to become my wife.'

He took a step closer and she felt her shoulders tense, priming her for his next move.

'You told me earlier that I needed to commit. And I have...'

He paused and her skin seemed to catch fire as, reaching out, he stroked the curve of her cheek gently.

'But in return you need to stop fighting me. That's only fair, isn't it?'

The rhythm of his fingers was making her breathing slow so that she felt as though she were suffocating.

'So when I politely suggest you go shopping, you go shopping,' he said softly. 'Or next time, I might not ask so nicely.'

And, leaving her furiously mouthing words after him, he turned and sauntered out of the room.

CHAPTER FOUR

'So…' Rollo paused and glanced over to where Daisy sat, slumped in one of the apartment's huge leather armchairs. 'You prefer coffee to tea, red wine to white and you hate whisky.'

He waited, letting a long silence pass, battling with an irritation that had become familiar to him over the last twenty-four hours.

'And…?' he prompted finally as she continued to stare across the living room, her gaze fixed determinedly on the view of downtown New York.

Turning, she screwed up her face as though concentrating. 'You like red wine too.' She hesitated. 'And you prefer your coffee white.'

He gritted his teeth. 'No. Black.'

Ordinarily he would have already drunk several cups of espresso. But right now he could do with something stronger.

They'd started early—cross-examining each other again and again until the answers felt automatic. Or that had been the plan. A muscle tightened in his jaw. Only instead of knuckling down, Daisy was acting like a teenager doing a detention.

'Oh, yeah. I remember now.' Stifling a yawn, she met his gaze, her brown eyes challenging him. 'Sorry.'

She didn't seem sorry. On the contrary, she sounded both unrepentant and bored.

Watching her shoulders slump in an exaggerated gesture of exhaustion, Rollo gritted his teeth but didn't reply. Instead, leaning back against the leather of the armchair, he studied her in silence, trying to decide just how to manage this new, modified version of Daisy.

Since yesterday, when he'd more or less ordered her to go shopping, she had stopped fighting him openly, choosing instead to treat him with the sort of forced politeness normally reserved for teachers or dull acquaintances.

It was driving him mad.

Yet, despite his irritation, there was something about her that got under his skin. He could feel himself responding to her defiance, her stubbornness…her beauty. Shifting against the cushions, he felt his pulse twitch. She *was* beautiful, but it was more than that. He'd dated a lot of women—models, actresses, socialites—all of them as beautiful and desirable as Daisy. And yet none of them had ever made him feel this way—so off balance, as though his calm, disciplined world had been tipped upside down. As though his life were not his own.

Which, of course, it wasn't any more.

Running his hand through his short, blonde hair, Rollo pressed his fingers into the base of his skull, where an ache was starting to form. In truth, it wouldn't be *his* life for the next twelve months— until after his marriage had ended in a quick, uncontested divorce. A marriage that hadn't even happened yet.

He breathed in sharply. Having always vowed to stay single, the fact that he was not only going to be married but divorced too blew his mind.

But there was no other way. He wanted that building, and he was going to keep his promise to his father—no matter what the cost to his sexual and mental health.

He frowned. Usually in life, and in business, he got what he wanted through a combination of persistence and money. But he'd been trying to buy this building for nearly ten years, and James Dunmore had made it clear that money wasn't the issue. He would only do business with a man who shared his values—a man who truly believed that family and marriage was the cornerstone of life.

It was easy for Dunmore to believe—*he* wasn't the one having to put his life on hold. Nor was he having to cohabit with a stubborn, sexy minx like Daisy Maddox, he thought irritably. Everything would be so much simpler and smoother if she were like every other woman he'd ever met. Eager, accommodating, flirty. But the woman he'd picked to be his first—his only—wife seemed determined to challenge him at every opportunity.

Even when he kissed her.

Especially when he kissed her.

His breath swelled in his throat, and just like that he could remember how it had felt when her lips had touched his. How she'd come alive in his arms, her body melting into his, hands tangling through his hair, her feverish response matching his desperate desire—

He let out a shallow breath. It was an image he needed little effort to remember, having spent the night replaying it inside his head, his frustration magnified by the fact that the cause of his discomfort was on the other side of the wall, no doubt sleeping peacefully.

Unable to sleep himself, he had lain in the darkness, trying to piece together the fragments of nakedness that she had inadvertently revealed to him. The pale length of her neck and throat, gleaming beneath the harsh lights in his office, the curve of her bare shoulder when she had fallen asleep on the sofa. To that he'd added the scab on her knee she'd got breaking into his office—glimpsed as she'd slid past him on the landing in the T-shirt she wore as a nightie.

He'd picked at those memories until just before dawn when, finally, he had fallen asleep.

Feeling her gaze on the side of his face, he pushed aside the burn of frustration in his groin and forced himself to concentrate instead on the thankfully fully clothed Daisy sitting opposite him.

'This is boring for both of us,' he said slowly. 'But the more committed you are to getting it right, the quicker we can move on.'

Daisy's brown eyes focused on Rollo's face. He was speaking to her as though she were a child. She felt her cheeks grow hot.

She shrugged. 'So I forgot? Big deal. It's not like anyone's going to be testing us.'

Last night, after his snooty remarks about her clothing, she had expended so much energy on hating him that she had instantly fallen into a heavy, dreamless sleep. Waking, she had felt calmer, determined to find a better way of managing him. Given that so far every confrontation had ended badly—*for her*—she'd resolved not to lose her temper. But it was going to be a hard challenge if he carried on being so aggravating.

'I'm an actress,' she said stiffly. 'I know what I have to do to get into character.'

'Then stop sulking and do it. It was you, after all, who told me that I had to commit to the role. Perhaps you should follow your own advice.'

He gave her a patronising smile that made her want to smother him with one of the sofa cushions. But instead she took a shallow breath and in her calmest voice said, 'It just feels so soulless and scripted. Couldn't we just hang out together and talk? That way we'd still get to know each other, only it would be more…' she searched for the right word '…more *organic*.'

It was a reasonable request. More reasonable, say, than demanding someone replace their entire wardrobe of clothes. But clearly being reasonable was not a concept that was familiar to Rollo.

Fuming silently, she watched him shake his head.

'Testing each other is the quickest way to learn

this stuff. Then we can go out and start putting it all into practice. In public.'

The thought of actually appearing in public as his girlfriend made panic skim across her skin like a stone. She glanced across to where he sat, lounging lazily in an armchair. Even dressed casually, in a faded T-shirt and jeans, he radiated both superiority and authority—the sort of undefinable power that went hand in hand with being an alpha male.

Her breath crowded in her throat as his gaze wandered casually over her face, down over the long white hippyish dress she had bought on holiday with David last year.

But what about *her*? She hardly qualified as a member of the elite. She had no job, no money and right now a future that didn't even really belong to her. Changing her clothes wasn't about to change any of those facts.

She lifted her chin. But why should she change, anyway? She wasn't ashamed of who she was or where she came from.

'Good,' she said, with something of her usual spirit. 'The sooner we can get on with this charade, the sooner it will all be over. I just wish it didn't feel so much like school.' She sighed. 'It reminds me of cramming for exams.'

'It does?' he said slowly, giving her one of his cool, blank looks. 'Interesting. I wouldn't have had you down as the swotty type.'

His green eyes were locked on to hers, taunting her. She opened her mouth to protest and then closed it again. It would be so gratifying to tell him that she'd been an A-grade student. That the library had been her second home. But she didn't think there was much chance of convincing him.

Mostly because it wasn't true.

'I suppose you were the top of the class?' She felt her cheeks grow warm as he surveyed her steadily.

'If you mean I worked hard, then, yes. But I made sure I had plenty of energy left for...*extra-curricular activities*.'

He gave her a slow, suggestive smile that curled like smoke around her throat. Her heart was banging high up in her ribs and, swallowing, she forced down the traitorous heat rising up inside her.

'Fascinating though it is to hear about your school days, we should probably press on,' she said stiffly. 'I might just get a glass of water first.'

And, standing up, she stalked across the room and into the kitchen.

Rollo watched her leave, his groin hardening as his gaze locked on to the swaying hips beneath her flimsy dress. Clearly, despite having gone shopping, she was determined to wear her own clothes when they were at home.

He shook his head, exasperated by her need to make a stand, and yet part of him—the part of him that would have dug in his heels in exactly the same way—couldn't help admiring her.

That didn't mean there wasn't plenty of room for improvement, he thought caustically. Not least in her laissez-faire attitude to the business of becoming his wife. Maybe it was time to remind her of what was at stake here…

In the kitchen, Daisy stared blankly at the gleaming white cupboards. Her mind was tumbling, but that was nothing to the chaos of her body. Her legs felt shaky and a dark, dragging ache like a bruise was spreading out inside her.

Why did he have this effect on her? Or rather, why *still*? Back in his office, she'd put it down to a combination of adrenaline and heightened emotion. So why was it happening *now*?

Taking a glass from one of the cupboards, she turned on the tap, watching the water splash into the stainless steel sink. If only she could slip away down the plughole too, she thought dully, filling her glass. If only she could escape so effortlessly.

But who was she escaping from? Rollo or herself?

'There's bottled water in the fridge, if you'd prefer. Still and sparkling.'

She tensed, her heartbeat stalling in her chest.

Not him. Not here and definitely not now. She wasn't ready.

She'd been hoping for a few much-needed moments alone to pull herself together, to talk some sense into what supposedly passed as her brain. But of course, as with everything else in her life since Rollo had walked into it, her hopes were subject to his will.

Turning, she felt her breath catch fire in her throat. He was standing in front of her, closer than she'd thought he would be…so close she could see the flecks of bronze in his eyes.

He was too close for comfort.

Only time would show if it was too close for her self-control.

She smiled tightly. 'No, I'm fine with tap.'

He stared at her unblinkingly and she felt her pulse plateau. He was stupidly handsome, and being so close to him was making her stupid. Why else would she feel so frantic to kiss him? Her cheeks were hot and, desperate to stop the woman in her responding to his blatant masculinity, she switched into waitress mode.

'I'm sorry, I didn't ask. Did you want anything?' She couldn't resist. 'White coffee? Sorry, I mean black.'

There was a short, quivering silence and then, tilting his head, he gave her a long, steady look. He shook his head. 'No, thanks. I'm trying to cut back.' The corners of his eyes creased. 'Just in case you didn't notice—that was unscripted.'

She looked up at him uncertainly. His mood seemed to have lightened and she could feel herself responding, her tension easing, so that for one off-balance moment she wanted to smile. And to see him smile back.

Except that if he smiled she was scared of what might happen. A smile might seem innocuous. Like tiptoeing onto a frozen lake. But at some point the ice would crack and suddenly she would be out of her depth.

Feeling his eyes on her face, she looked up and met his gaze coolly. At least she hoped she looked cool. She certainly didn't want him guessing her real thoughts.

'I'm not trying to be difficult,' she said slowly. 'Truly. But you're treating this—*us*—like some kind of equation. We can't pull this off by just joining all the dots. We need to try and make our relationship feel as natural as possible. And that's not going to happen if we just sit here parroting facts to one another.'

It had to be the strangest conversation she had ever had. Only in some ways, wasn't it liberating to be able to talk so openly about what she wanted? About what it would take to make their relationship work? With all her previous boyfriends she'd just tried to second-guess everything and failed. Spectacularly. But because she wasn't in love with Rollo, and never would be, she didn't care about speaking her mind.

Half expecting him to argue with her, she was surprised when instead, he nodded.

'That makes sense.'

He sounded interested—friendly, even—and as something like panic bubbled up inside her she realised too late that being near him had been a lot easier when all she had felt was hostility.

Particularly given that he clearly *deserved* her hostility.

Or she'd thought he had.

But as his eyes drifted gently over her skin like a haze of summer heat she realised that his charm was something she hadn't allowed herself to imagine. And, glancing up into his face, watching his beautiful hard features soften, she knew why: it was too dangerous! Especially when that almost smile was making it impossible for her to think rationally, so that suddenly she felt unsure of herself, unsure of how she should respond.

He was lounging against the worktop, his eyes watching her intently in a way that she didn't fully understand. All she knew was that it made her feel hot and helplessly wound up.

'We can make this work, Daisy.'

She nodded, panic muting her.

'It's very new for both of us. Try and think of it as just another job.'

Frowning, she found her voice. 'But it's not like that at all. When I'm acting I learn my lines and get into character. But only when I'm on stage. I don't act like Lady Macbeth at home.'

His gaze was steady and unblinking. 'That's a relief,' he said softly.

His voice sent goosebumps over her skin and she felt a sharp, gnawing heat inside, like the first flames of a forest fire. She knew she had blushed and she wanted to look away, but she couldn't move. Instead she held her breath, heart hammering, trying to quiet the turmoil in her body.

Breathing out, she said quickly, 'It's just… We're supposed to be madly in love.'

Something shifted in the room—a loosening of tension like the wind dropping. For a moment they stared at one another, and then his hand came up, his fingers smoothing over her cheeks, his touch firm yet tender.

'Supposed to be, yes.' His hand dropped and he took a step back, his green eyes shadowed and still.

She swallowed, her breath cartwheeling inside her chest. 'So we need some…' She paused.

She'd been about to say *romance*, or *passion*. But passion was clearly a complication she didn't need to introduce into their relationship. Not if her body's intense but dangerous response to him was anything to go by. And, as for romance, she wasn't sure he actually understood the meaning of the word.

She frowned. 'We need to have some fun.'

His mouth curved. 'Fun?'

Daisy gazed at him. Was that an alien concept to him too?

'Yes. *Fun.* We need fun. Not facts. Let's get out of here and go somewhere we can talk and chill.'

For a moment she thought he wasn't going to answer. That maybe he hadn't even been listening.

'I see...'

The change in him was barely discernible. His voice was perfectly calm and even, but she could sense an indecision in him that she had never seen before.

'I keep a box at the Met Opera.' He pulled out his phone. 'I don't actually know what's on, but I'm sure you'll enjoy it and it's completely private. I'll get my PA to notify the theatre.'

She stared at him numbly. Clearly he hadn't been listening. Or why would he suggest a night at the opera? It was hardly the most laid-back way to spend an evening—nor would they even be able to talk. It was probably just somewhere he took whatever woman he happened to be seeing at the time.

Pushing aside the niggle of pain that thought caused, she glared at him coldly. 'I wouldn't want you to put yourself out. Besides, I don't like opera.'

His eyes jerked up to hers, their expression so cold and hostile that instantly her muscles tautened for flight.

There was a long hiss of silence.

Rollo stared at her coldly. Anger was blanking his brain, so that for a moment he couldn't speak—

and besides, he needed the time to bank down his fury. Not just with Daisy for her rudeness, but with himself for trying to meet her halfway.

For being weak.

Keeping his eyes unfocused, he stared past her until finally he could trust his voice.

'In that case, I'll leave you to get on with learning your lines.'

It took her a moment to understand what he was saying. 'What do you mean? Are you going somewhere?'

'To the office.'

She felt his words scoop out a hollow at the bottom of her stomach.

'The office? But I thought you wanted to—'

'Then you made a mistake. As I did.' A muscle flickered at his jawline. 'But on the plus side, at least we really *are* getting to know each other.'

He turned and crossed the room in three long strides.

Daisy let out a short jerky breath. She wasn't quite sure what had just happened. But the emptiness of the room was doing something strange to her body—making her pulse race too fast so that suddenly she needed to do something with her hands.

Picking up her glass, she rinsed it out and started drying it furiously.

His words were rolling round her head like marbles in a jar. What kind of person upped and went to work in the middle of an argument? And then abruptly the marbles stilled.

Going to the office? But why the hell was he going into the office? It was Sunday.

Slumped behind his desk, Rollo stared bleakly out of the window at the city he called home. To the left was the past: the building where he'd grown up—the building he'd been trying to buy from James Dunmore for all of his adult life. To the right lay his future: the penthouse where he was living with Daisy. And, whichever way he looked at it, he needed one in order to acquire the other.

He wasn't regretting his decision to coerce Daisy into being his wife so much as reassessing it. Having overridden her objections, he had thought it would be just as easy to maintain her cooperation.

But, remembering her expression when he'd offered to take her to the opera, he felt a twist of anger low in his stomach. He should have just told her how it was going to be. Instead, driven by some inexplicable need to make their relationship more natural, more spontaneous, he'd let down his guard.

Let himself be manipulated, more like.

He gritted his teeth. A long time ago, he had sworn never to make himself vulnerable like that. Never to become his father—a man who had spent a lifetime trying and failing to please one woman.

Only he'd broken his own rules.

And there was nobody to blame but himself.

Daisy might be all soft brown eyes and seductive curves, but she was also a nightmare on legs. Devious. Wilful. Utterly untrustworthy. And that assessment didn't even take into account her ability as an actress to slip between multiple personas—one minute, a warrior queen, standing her ground in his office, the next, falling asleep on his sofa like an overtired child.

But was he marrying all of them or one of them?

A small draught swept across his shoulders and he heard the door to his office open softly. Around him the air seemed to ripple and tighten, and he knew without even looking round that it was Daisy.

The light through the window lit up her face and he was struck again by her luminous beauty. But not enough to break the uneasy silence that was filling his office.

'Your doorman let me in,' she said finally.

Her voice was brittle, like an eggshell, and she gave him a small, tight smile.

'He recognised me from the other night.'

He nodded.

She bit her lip. 'I can go if you want...' Her voice trailed off.

He watched her hovering in the doorway. A different Daisy again—not defiant or afraid so much as apprehensive.

'Why are you here?' There was no inflection in his voice.

'It's almost three o'clock.'

He heard her swallow.

'You didn't eat much breakfast.'

Her face was still.

'And then you didn't come back for lunch. So I brought you some food.'

Hesitantly she held up a brown paper bag.

Her eyes were searching his face and he realised that she was worried—worried about *him*—and shock spread slowly over his chest like a bruise.

'It's pizza. Four cheeses with extra olives. And a margherita.' She breathed out. 'I remembered.'

She made a small, shapeless gesture with her hand and set the bag down on the floor. Edging backwards, she said quickly, 'Anyway, I'll just leave it here and if you feel hungry later—'

'Did they use pecorino or Parmigiana?'

Daisy stopped. Her pulse quivered.

'Pecorino.'

'Light or heavy on the sauce?'

She swallowed.

'Light.'

'Okay.'

He was studying her face, his green eyes utterly unreadable. She held her breath until finally he held out his hand.

'Do you want to eat here or in the boardroom?'

In the end they decided to stay in his office, sitting at either end of the sofa with the pizza boxes between them.

'I've never had four cheeses before,' she said, nibbling a string of mozzarella into her mouth. 'I thought it would be too—'

'Cheesy?'

She almost smiled. '*No*. Too dairy! But it's actually not.'

They talked randomly. Nothing personal. Just about food and New York. But all the tension of the past two days seemed to have vanished. Finally he picked up the empty boxes, folded them in half and slid them back into the bag.

'I think that's probably the best pizza I've ever eaten. Where did you get it?'

Daisy felt a spasm of happiness shoot through her. It felt so much lighter, looser between them—normal, almost.

'Oh, there's this really great family-run pizzeria near David's apartment.'

Rollo frowned. 'Your brother's apartment? That's a bit of a trip from here.'

'I suppose so. But I was out walking anyway.'

She glanced past him, colour rising on her face.

After Rollo had left she had been too angry and thwarted and confused to sit down. Instead she had paced round the apartment like an animal at the zoo. But pacing and anger were hard to sustain, and after an hour or so, her strides had started to shorten, her anger fading, until finally she'd stopped walking and sat down.

She'd felt miserable. And guilty. No doubt Rollo had thought that arranging an evening at the opera—just the two of them in a private box—would be the perfect way to spend some time alone together. And, remembering that moment of uncharacteristic irresolution before he'd spoken, she'd felt her stomach drop.

It had been a peace offering.

Only she had thrown it back in his face.

Worse, she'd been so busy resenting him that she'd focused entirely on why their relationship should fail when she should have been finding ways to make it work.

She shifted uncomfortably on the sofa.

'I always go for a walk when I'm upset. You know, when I need to think.' Her eyes flickered past him. 'It's just all of this—us—it's harder than I thought. And I think it's going to get harder when I have to start lying to people. Not strangers…I mean my parents and David. But that's my problem, not yours—'

'That makes it my problem too.'

He was silent a moment, then he said quietly, 'Are you worried they won't approve of me?'

Her eyes widened with disbelief. 'No, I'm worried they *will*. They're going to be so happy for me—and I don't deserve it. It makes me feel cruel.'

'You're not cruel.' His face searched her face, eyes softening a fraction. 'You're here for your brother. That makes you loyal. And strong. It takes a lot of courage to do what you're doing.'

Was that a compliment? She stared at him, confused. 'Or stupidity.'

'I don't think you're stupid.'

She grimaced. 'You never read my school reports. "Could do better" was a fairly universal theme.'

'That's got more to do with your attitude than your aptitude.'

His voice was oddly gentle and, looking up, she saw he was leaning slightly forward, his expression carefully casual.

'Maybe a little.' She smiled weakly. 'But David's the smart one. He's, like, a genius at maths and science. But he paints amazingly too—and he loves the opera—' Her heartbeat gave a guilty little lurch.

'Perhaps I should have invited him.'

She shivered, half choked on her breath, cleared her throat. 'About that—' She shifted uncomfortably on the sofa. 'What I said to you about opera. It was rude and unnecessary and I'm sorry.'

There was a fraction of a pause and then she felt his gaze sweep over her like a searchlight.

'I'm guessing you had a bad experience with *The Ring Cycle.*'

She gazed at him blankly. 'The what?'

'*Der Ring des Nibelungen* by Wagner. Lasts about fifteen hours. I thought it might be why you hate opera.'

She shuddered. 'Is that what we were going to watch?'

Shaking his head, he smiled—a smile so sweet, so irresistible, that Daisy instantly forgot all her misery and confusion.

'No. I wouldn't inflict that on my worst enemy.'

'Well, speaking as your worst enemy, I'm very grateful,' she said lightly.

His smile faded. 'You're not my worst enemy.'

Daisy gazed up at him. His eyes were focused on her face, so clear and green and deep that suddenly she wanted to dive in and drown in them.

'But you hate me…' For some reason she didn't understand her voice was shaking, the words dancing away from her like leaves on the wind.

Leaning towards her, he lifted his hand and touched her cheek. 'I don't hate you,' he said softly.

Her heart was somersaulting in her chest. It was lucky she was sitting down, because she could feel that gravity had stopped working and if she were standing up, she would simply have floated away.

His hand was tracing the line of her jaw, his thumb gently stroking the skin. She sat still and mute, hypnotised both by the tenderness of his touch and his fierce, shimmering gaze. Around her the walls were tilting inwards, spinning slowly.

Throat drying, she took a quick, jagged breath like a gasp. 'I don't hate you either.'

Suddenly she couldn't be so close to him and not touch him back and, reaching out, she put a hand on his arm. His skin felt smooth and warm, like carved wood. But it was his mouth—that beautiful, curving mouth—that made her body quiver, a hot, humid tension building inside her like a summer storm.

She breathed out softly. 'I didn't bring any dessert.'

His eyes locked on to hers and they stared at one another in silence. And then he dropped his gaze and, glancing down at his wrist, said quietly, 'It's late. We should head home.'

As they stood in the corridor, waiting for the lift, Daisy felt his gaze on the side of her face. 'What is it? Did you forget something?'

He shook his head. 'No.'

He paused and she felt that tension again—that indecision.

'Thanks for the pizza. It was fun.' Frowning, he cleared his throat. 'I just want you to know that

I didn't suggest we go to the opera just because I have a box.'

She nodded dumbly.

There was clearly more to his words than their literal meaning, and part of her badly wanted to question him further. But instead she simply reached out and took his hand. 'And I want you to know that you don't have to worry. We can make this work.'

She felt his surprise and braced herself, expecting him to pull away. But after a moment his fingers tightened around hers, and as they stepped into the lift together she breathed out softly.

It might not be happy-ever-after, but it was a truce of sorts.

CHAPTER FIVE

'GOOD MORNING, MS MADDOX. I'm Kate and I'll be your personal therapist this morning.'

Looking up, Daisy smiled apprehensively at the slim young woman standing in front of her. Back at home she'd had manicures and the occasional facial. But the Tahara Sanctuary was one of New York's most exclusive spas. Everything oozed sophistication and exclusivity. In fact, it was so exclusive that she had an entire relaxation suite just to herself.

An hour and a half later Daisy was starting to understand why wealthy people always looked so relaxed. After a salt-and-mint-oil exfoliation and a cleansing herbal bath, she was now enjoying her first ever full-body massage and could feel her stresses dissolving beneath Kate's expert touch.

Stifling a yawn, Daisy closed her eyes as from somewhere across the room she heard a soft tap at the door. There was a slight shift in the atmosphere, the cool air mixing with the fragranced heat of the room, and then her body tensed.

An electric prickle rippled over her skin as she heard Kate say eagerly, 'Oh, Mr Fleming. How lovely to see you again.'

Her eyes snapped open, and the next moment her heart lurched sideways as she heard a familiar deep voice say casually, 'It's nice to see you too, Kate.'

Pulse hammering against her skin, Daisy held her breath, painfully aware she was naked except for a pair of panties and a towel folded across her bottom and thighs.

Since suspending hostilities with Rollo, over a week ago, she'd actually begun to enjoy herself. In part, it was because she'd stopped feeling that being happy was somehow a betrayal of David. And in part because her new A-list life was quite hard to resist. But the main reason was that, oddly, being with Rollo was by far the easiest relationship she'd ever had.

Not just because he'd kept his word and had stopped picking on her. Or because he was smart, sophisticated and stupidly handsome—although that helped. Truthfully, it was the first time she'd ever really felt free to be herself with a man. With Rollo, she didn't have to worry about her heart or the future. She could just sit back and enjoy the ride.

Although that theory had seemed a lot more convincing when she wasn't lying almost naked on a bed in front of him.

Something cool slipped over her neck and down her bare back, and she knew as surely as if she was looking at him that he was watching her. Pushing away an almost overwhelming impulse to yank the towel up over her body and hide from his scrutiny, she said as casually as she could manage, 'I didn't know you were going to pop in.'

There. She'd done it. It wasn't a ticker-tape parade, but they were now officially a couple. It felt strange, but exciting. Of course, Rollo's personal household staff had seen them together but somehow having Kate there made it feel more real.

'Oh, you know me, darling. Always acting on impulse. I hope I haven't disturbed you.'

The teasing note in his voice as much as the unfamiliar term of endearment made her pulse twitch and her heart pound. She lifted her head slowly.

He was standing beside her, his beautiful sculpted face lit up with mockery and amusement, and nervously she wondered why he was there.

Hoping she looked less flustered than she felt, she shook her head and smiled. 'Not at all.'

'Excellent—well, you're in good hands.'

Next to her, Daisy felt rather than saw the young therapist blush. Rollo's eyes, however, were fixed so intently on hers that for a moment it felt as if they were alone.

With an effort, she dragged her gaze towards Kate and smiled. 'Very good hands. I feel completely relaxed.'

'That's good. I know you've been a little stressed lately.'

He *should* know, she thought with a flash of irritation, since he was the prime cause of the stress. But, gritting her teeth, she said crisply, 'A little. But there's been quite a lot going on.'

'A lot of our clients suffer from stress-related conditions,' Kate said earnestly. 'Muscle pain, breathlessness, headaches, insomnia—it can even cause loss of libido.'

'Is that right?' Rollo said softly. 'We can't have that, can we...*darling*?'

The heat and the perfumed air were filling his head. But that wasn't why his brain was working at half speed.

What was he doing here? he wondered dazedly.

But watching Daisy's pupils widen, the black swallowing the brown, he felt his body throb with desire and knew that the answer to his question was lying in front of him.

He was supposed to be on a conference call. Only on his way back to the office he'd glanced out of the window and noticed a pizza delivery scooter—bright red, with a big cooler box clamped behind the seat. Instantly he'd thought of Daisy, and before he'd known what he was doing he'd told his driver to divert to the spa.

But he'd needed to see her, he reassured himself. To tell her about the party at the gallery and give her time to get used to the idea. After all, tonight would be their first public outing.

Feeling calmer, he smiled lazily down at her. 'Maybe I need to help you relax more. Perhaps I could learn how to massage.'

Daisy froze. There was something in his voice that made her breath dissolve in her throat.

Summoning up a careless smile, she said quickly, 'That's so sweet of you. But you don't need to do anything, *darling*. Kate's taking care of me.'

Rollo stared down at her assessingly. 'Yes, she is,' he murmured. 'But then Kate doesn't know you like I do. She doesn't know your weaknesses.'

His eyes roamed over her naked back.

'In fact, you know what? I think I've got this, Kate,' she heard him say quietly, and then she tensed, her body straining like a sail in a high wind, as across the room she heard the door open and click shut.

'I don't think this—' she began. But her protesting words dried up in her mouth as she felt his warm hand slide gently down her back.

Suddenly it was as though she was unravelling, his fingers untying every nerve, loosening her resistance and her willpower.

She watched dazedly as he reached down and picked up an open jar.

'Mandarin butter. Sounds delicious.' Scanning the label, he smiled slowly, so that her heart began to bang violently against her ribs.

'Apparently it releases the body into a state of euphoria. What's not to like?' he murmured as his fingers splayed out over her shoulders and heat flared over her skin like a gunpowder trail catching fire.

Daisy shivered, the bruising ache in her pelvis muting the alarm bells inside her head. His hands were gentle and firm, their warmth melting the butter. But it wasn't only the butter that was melting. A liquid heat was seeping through her body, her insides were growing hot and tight, and her muscles were tensing around the ache that was spreading out with a slowness that made her want to moan out loud.

Her heart started to pound. *Don't just lie here. Get up. Tell him to leave. Tell him to stop touching you*, she told herself desperately.

But, like someone in shock, she could only lower her head, her limbs growing heavier, blood thickening and slowing like treacle, her skin twitching restlessly beneath his touch. Her eyes fluttered and closed.

He didn't need to learn how to massage, she thought dizzily, a shiver passing down her spine as his hands rippled over her body. He already knew exactly how to touch. And where...

Staring down at the pale curve of Daisy's back, Rollo watched the pulse throbbing beneath her skin like a trapped moth and felt his body grow hard— painfully hard.

He'd expected her to be having some kind of beauty treatment. It was a spa, after all. But he hadn't expected to find her on a bed, her naked body barely covered. Glancing down, he rested his gaze on the jutting sweep of her bottom, pushing against the towel, and lust ripped through him like a train.

She was so beautiful—and he wanted her so badly.

Unable to stop himself, he lengthened his strokes, caressing lower and lower still—until, with the breath twisting in his throat, he pressed his thumbs into the cleft at the base of her spine, his groin tightening as he felt her body shudder and arch upwards.

'Rollo!'

Her voice—raw, husky, shivering with desire—broke into his passion-clogged brain like a thunderclap.

What the hell was he playing at?

He'd been on the verge of pulling her into his arms and letting his hands and mouth roam freely over that satin-soft skin.

His heart jolted forward. His blood was humming, his body taut, straining with desire like some hormonal teenage boy, and there was nobody to blame but himself. From the moment in his office when she'd looked up at him, dazed but defiant, he'd wanted her. And, as with every other woman in his life, he'd assumed that he was in

control. That he could contain the chaos she'd un-
leashed inside him.

But when he'd walked into the spa the sexual tension between them had been like a brutal punch to
the face. Seeing her on that bed had knocked everything out of his head except the need to touch
her. A need so primal and intense that he'd been
incapable of doing anything but respond to it.

His pulse shivered and, fighting against the excruciating sting of frustration in his groin, he ran
a finger lightly up over her spine to the base of her
neck. Pushing aside the loose knot of blonde hair,
he watched as her eyelashes fluttered open.

'I think that might be enough euphoria for one
day. Unless, of course, you'd like me to do your
front, as well?'

His eyes rested on her face, his gaze so intent, so
intimate that suddenly she felt a teasing heat tiptoe
over her body like a ballerina en pointe.

She stared at him mutely—dazed, almost
drugged by the shivering heat spilling over her
skin.

Remembering how she had moaned his name,
she felt her cheeks grow hot. Had he heard? Did
he know the effect he'd had on her?

Meeting his cool, assessing gaze, she felt her stomach tense.

Of course he did!

Which was why she should never have let him touch her. Only it was too late to start having regrets now.

Aware that he was still watching her, and hoping he hadn't guessed quite how much her body had revelled in his touch, she gritted her teeth and gave him a quick, tight smile.

'I think I'll pass.' She glanced pointedly past him to the door. 'Kate will be coming back any moment. She's going to give me a facial.'

According to Kate, it would help clear her skin of toxins. Her chest squeezed tight. If only it would also purge her body of this stupid and inappropriate physical attraction she appeared to have for Rollo. Not that anything was going to happen, she told herself firmly. She might have agreed to call a truce, but that didn't mean she was going to have sex with him.

Sleeping with Rollo would be a mistake—and she'd already made quite enough of those. Maybe if their situation had been different, she might have considered exploring the chemistry between them. But she could hardly ignore the fact that he was blackmailing her. And, besides, she wasn't about to do anything to jeopardise the entente cordiale between them.

Logic demanded that she override her hormones. It would be a lot easier though if her brain and body both felt the same way about him.

Or better still felt nothing at all.

Suddenly she was desperate to leave—to escape Rollo's unsettling presence and the spiralling tensions in the room—and, reaching down, cheeks burning, she snatched the towel, pulling it swiftly up to cover her naked breasts.

'Actually, I should probably go and look for her. Would you mind passing me my robe?'

He held it out to her, his fingers curling loosely in the soft fabric, and her heart started to beat faster as she remembered how freely and recently those same hands had roved over her body.

His green eyes lightened with amusement as she pushed her arms into the sleeves, trying to cover herself up as quickly as possible.

'Relax,' he said softly. 'I'm not in the habit of jumping women. Besides, I've got a meeting with my head of finance—and, much as I'd love to give it a miss, I can't just turn my back on work. Otherwise…' pausing, he gave her a slow, curling smile

'...I might not have a business left for when we finally convince Dunmore to sell to me?'

Sliding off the bed, disconcerted by his sudden, blunt reminder of why she was in his life, Daisy tried to match his smile. 'Okay. Then I'll see you later.'

He frowned. 'Actually, a little earlier than that. There's been a change of plan. That's why I dropped in.'

His eyes rested calmly on her face and Daisy was jolted back into reality. Of course, there had been a reason for his visit. Hard-headed businessmen like Rollo didn't do random or impulsive.

Ignoring the prickling disappointment inside her chest, she met his gaze. 'Why earlier?' she said stiffly.

'We're going out tonight,' he said coolly. 'To a gallery. I meant to say something before, only I got a little distracted.'

She nodded. But her brain was seething with resentment. He was so autocratic—taking it for granted that she had no plans, or none that couldn't be rearranged to suit his agenda.

'The limo will pick us up at seven. That should give you plenty of time to get ready.'

He spoke with the same brisk detachment he

used for discussing the logistics of his day with his driver, Kenny, and he was walking towards the door before she finally managed to speak.

'Tonight?'

He nodded. 'It's an exhibition. I'm a patron at the gallery and they're having a party.'

Daisy stared at him in horror. 'But what about my parents and David? They don't know anything about us.'

'That won't change. It's a small, private gallery. Local paparazzi will pick it up, but I doubt it'll make the national news.'

She lifted her chin. 'But you said we wouldn't be ready for another week—'

His eyes drifted mockingly over her flushed cheeks. 'I think we're ready. Don't you?'

She met his gaze. Her skin was still tingling from the heat of his touch, her body quivering like a city after an earthquake, and she knew that she must look dazed, feverish. *Turned on.* So, yes, they were ready.

Not that it mattered either way, she thought as the door closed behind him. Judging by Rollo's expression, she was going to be at that party— ready or not.

* * *

Only another two minutes and it would be showtime!

Glancing furtively at the screen on her phone, Daisy felt a familiar rush of nerves—the mixture of excitement tinged with fear and dread that preceded every first night. Tasting the adrenaline in her mouth, she shuddered involuntarily.

'Are you cold?'

She jerked her head around and glanced up at Rollo. She had almost forgotten he was there—which seemed incredible, given that she was sitting next to him in *his* limousine. But it was always the same before any performance: she had to lose herself in the fear, let the panic swamp her, before she faced her audience.

She shook her head. 'No. It's just nerves. I always get them—' Suddenly aware that Rollo was unlikely to be interested in her stage fright, she broke off.

But instead of turning away, he stared at her levelly. 'You're scared?'

'Yes.' She sighed. 'But I need to be.' Seeing his gaze sharpen, she felt colour suffuse her cheeks. 'I know it sounds crazy.'

'It's not crazy. It's biology.' Reaching out, he laid

his hand over hers. 'Fear is important. It warns us of danger.'

Her heart squeezed. If that was the case, then why wasn't she pushing his hand away? Or climbing into the boot? Or anywhere Rollo wasn't?

Glancing over, she felt her breath dissolve in her throat. Up close in the limo, his beauty was almost intimidating. He was so perfect, so glamorous, with that fringe of eyelashes grazing the curve of his cheekbones. His dark suit accentuated his broad shoulders and lean torso, and above a pale yellow shirt his eyes were as green and intoxicating as absinthe.

Smiling perfunctorily, she turned to the window—away from the dazzling symmetry of his face.

It was so confusing. He was the bad guy—the villain. She wasn't supposed to like him. And it had been easy not to like him when he'd been brutal and ruthless. But it was harder when he held her hand so gently. Hard too, to pretend that she wasn't enjoying being half of a beautiful couple.

She breathed out. Everything was so much simpler when they fought. At least then her feelings were straightforward. Now, though, she felt increasingly unsure of herself—particularly when she was sitting so close to him.

His fingers slipped around her wrist. 'Your pulse is racing,' he said softly.

'It's because I'm not breathing properly,' she said quickly. 'I need more oxygen.'

His eyes gleamed. 'A science lesson on the way to an art gallery? What's next? Spelling? Long division?'

She had to stop her mouth from curving up at the corners. 'It's just biology. And I'm sure you don't need me to teach you anything about *that*.'

His eyes locked on to hers. 'I bet you say that to all the men.'

'Actually, no,' she said crisply. 'Only you.'

After she'd come so close to losing control at the spa, she was trying to keep her distance. But it was difficult with the hard length of his thigh pressing against hers.

He smiled. 'So you're nervous. What can I do to help?'

She gazed at him in exasperation. '*You?* What could *you* do? You're the reason I'm nervous.'

His fingers stilled against her skin and there was a thick beat of silence. Staring past him, Daisy swallowed. Her cheeks felt hot. She was tingling all over.

'I make you nervous?'

'Not you,' she managed finally. 'This. Us.' Even to her ears her denial sounded unconvincing, and she felt her face grow hotter. 'I mean, us being out together in public. It makes me nervous. You, I can handle.'

Her heart was pounding. Who was she trying to kid? She might just as well say she could handle an escaped lion.

She met his gaze defiantly and instantly wished she hadn't, for he was watching her lazily, a hint of a smile tugging at the curve of his mouth.

'Is that right?'

Colour spread like spilt wine over her throat and collarbone, but thankfully there was no time to come up with a sensible answer because the car was pulling up outside a pale grey building. Suddenly there was a jostle of photographers, and flashbulbs exploded against the windows of the limo.

Inside the gallery everything was cool and quiet. A pianist was playing some familiar jazz tunes, and immaculately groomed men and women were drifting around in pairs and groups, stopping to sip champagne and gaze at the paintings.

Or rather they had been looking at the paintings.

Daisy felt her whole body grow rigid.

Now they all seemed to be gazing at her and Rollo.

'Relax. You look beautiful.'

His voice was soft, and she felt his fingers tighten around hers as she glanced down at her dark blue dress.

'Maybe it's too much?'

His gaze flickered over her bare shoulders. 'Any less and I don't think I could be held responsible for my actions.' He smiled. 'Don't worry about everyone else. They're just curious. They don't bite.'

'You make them sound like goats,' she muttered.

He laughed out loud. 'Now you come to mention it, there is a certain resemblance.'

At the start of the evening Daisy had been anxious that she would feel out of place. Many of the guests were recognisable from television and the newspapers. But it was surprisingly easy to feel confident with Rollo's arm wrapped loosely around her waist. What was harder was remembering that she was there as part of some elaborate deception.

Not that anyone else would have known that was

what she was thinking. She smiled and nodded and made small talk. But she was barely aware of anything except the steady pressure of his hand, and of how her body was responding to it, to him, to his charm and the sound of his voice.

Her pulse jumped. Surely that was a *good* thing. After all, she was supposed to be acting as though she was hopelessly in love with him. *So act*, she told herself firmly. And, leaning in towards him, she let her arm brush against the hard muscles of his chest.

'Shall we go and have a look around?' she said softly.

Despite never really having understood art, she found the paintings both interesting and beautiful. One in particular was mesmerising: a rippling wave of green and red and black done in oils.

'Striking, isn't it?'

A slim, elderly woman was standing beside her, gazing critically at the canvas.

Daisy nodded. 'They're all incredible. This is the one I'd buy though.'

But only in her dreams. According to the catalogue, the painting cost more than she'd earned last year.

Next to her, the woman who'd spoken held out her hand. 'Bobbie Bayard.'

Daisy blinked. 'Daisy Maddox.'

'Which Maddox? Farming or finance?'

Daisy gazed at her in confusion.

'Neither.'

It was Rollo. Sliding his hand into Daisy's, he leaned forward and kissed the silver-haired woman on both cheeks.

'She's not from one of the old families, Bobbie, so you can stop digging.'

'Good.' Bobbie beamed. 'The old families are like me. Obsolete and withering away.'

Rollo shook his head. 'Ignore her,' he said to Daisy. 'She's not even close to withering. She was sitting in the front row at New York Fashion Week just three days ago. And she's got a sixth sense when it comes to picking up-and-coming artists.'

'I think I might have just met my match. Your girl's got a good eye.' Glancing approvingly at Daisy, Bobbie moved on to the next picture.

Your girl. Rollo's girl.

An electric current snaked across Daisy's skin. Looking up, she blinked. His eyes were fixed on her face, so dark and green and intent that she felt a cool, juddering shiver slip down her spine, like water dropping over rocks.

'So why do you like it?' he said finally.

Feeling her heart start to thump, she glanced back at the painting. 'I don't know. It makes me feel like I'm drowning. But not in a bad way. More like I don't have to fight any more.'

It made her feel oddly vulnerable, revealing something to Rollo so spontaneously.

'Then maybe you shouldn't,' he said quietly. 'Fight it, I mean.'

She gazed up at him mutely. The chatter and laughter around them faded away and suddenly she had the same sensation she'd had at the spa— that it was just the two of them, alone.

Rollo stared at her steadily, watching her eyes widen and soften. 'Maybe you should just give in...'

'So tell me, Rollo, just exactly how did you two meet?'

It was Bobbie. Head spinning, he turned as she looped her arm through his.

'That's a good question.'

He stared at her dazedly, trying to remember, his brain grasping for the right answer—the answer he and Daisy had agreed on. But it wasn't there, and he felt a blinding white-out of panic, his mind blank of everything except the moment he'd caught Daisy in his office. The one memory he couldn't actually use.

'I—I'm not sure,' he said slowly. 'Was it at work?'

Beside him he could feel eyes on his face. Only they weren't just Daisy's eyes any more. Around him he could feel the room shifting and shrinking, and he knew that soon the questions would get harder and everything would be so much worse.

'Yes, it was.' Daisy's voice was quiet but firm.

Glancing up, he saw she was smiling calmly at Bobbie, and some of the pressure eased inside his head.

'Rollo is trying to be discreet because he knows I don't like telling people I'm a waitress. But that's what I was doing the night we met. I'd done something stupid and he found a way to make it okay. But the weird thing was we'd already met.'

He stared at her. She was improvising her way back to their story, her eyes prompting him so that he heard himself say easily, 'Yes. We had. At a play. You see, Daisy's actually an actress.'

Rolling her eyes, Daisy shook her head. 'I trained to be an actress. And, yes, I was in a play. An awful play that was so off-Broadway it might as well have been in Pennsylvania. But Rollo was in the audience.'

'It wasn't that bad,' he said quietly.

Looking up at him, Daisy felt her insides tighten. His eyes were fierce, almost protective, and her breath stuttered in her throat as she forced herself to remember that he hadn't even been at that theatre. Had never seen her act.

'It's okay. You don't have to—'

'I'm not.'

He held her gaze and she stared at him in silence, hypnotised, her heart thudding, fear colliding with fascination.

'You were good. Better than good. You made people believe.'

Later, watching him talk to one of the artists, Daisy sifted through his words, twisting and rearranging them. Maybe he had meant what he said. But how could he when he had never seen her act? She glanced across the room. If anyone was good at acting, it was Rollo. Everybody believed in him, and more than anything they wanted him to believe in them.

But, of course, they did, she thought helplessly. Even surrounded by A-listers, he was movie star handsome, his charisma and poise matters of fact.

Not just something to be switched on for an audience.

Suddenly he looked up and met her gaze head-on. Her pulse leapfrogged over itself as she watched him make his excuses and saunter across the room.

'Seen enough?'

For one horrible moment she thought he was referring to himself. Then her brain clicked up a gear and she realised he was talking about the paintings.

She shrugged. 'I think so. But I'm happy to stay if you want.'

Gently he reached out and tipped up her chin. 'What I want is to be alone with you,' he said softly.

And then he smiled—a smile that warmed her skin like sunlight—and pulling her closer, he kissed her.

Around them the murmur of conversation slowed and quietened, but Daisy barely noticed. Eyes closing, stomach flipping over in helpless response to his probing tongue, she was only aware of the heat of his mouth and the hard length of his body pressing against her quivering belly. Hands curling into his shirt, she dragged him closer, kissing him back as her stomach muscles tensed around the tight, aching heat that was balling inside her.

It's just a job, she told herself dazedly. *You're a professional actress playing a role and this is all part of the performance.*

But as her hands rose and splayed against his chest somewhere in the back of her brain she knew that whatever was happening it was no longer just for show. It felt real—dangerously real...

Only there was no time to process that thought. She felt him shift against her, breaking the kiss. And, opening her eyes, she saw herself reflected in his gaze—small and still and stunned.

For a fraction of a second she thought she saw something flicker across his face. But she was too busy trying to hide her own reaction to really be sure, and then he was drawing her against him, guiding her towards the door.

Back at his apartment, the lights had been turned down, and in the living room there was a bottle of champagne chilling in an ice bucket.

Catching sight of her expression, Rollo raised an eyebrow. 'I wasn't sure how tonight would go. Champagne seemed like a good idea either way. Here.'

Popping the cork, he filled two glasses and handed one to Daisy.

'To us.'

'To us,' she echoed, her heart twitching as she remembered the kiss they'd shared in the gallery. 'So you're pleased with how it went?' she said tentatively, dropping her bag onto the sofa.

'Definitely. I think we aced it. Which reminds me…'

His eyes flickered past her and, turning, she saw a large, flat parcel wrapped in brown paper.

'I have something for you. A present.'

Stunned, speechless, she stared at the parcel in silence until finally, with a hint of impatience, Rollo said, 'Aren't you going to open it?"

'Y-yes. Of course,' she stammered.

Putting down her glass, she tugged clumsily at the paper and gasped. It was the painting from the gallery.

She gazed at it speechlessly. 'I don't—'

He frowned. 'You don't like it?'

'N-no, I do. I love it. But I can't possibly accept it—' Not when she knew how much it cost. Only it seemed ill-mannered to mention money.

He shrugged. 'Why not? You like it and I want to give it to you.'

She swallowed. He made it sound so easy. So

tempting. Looking up, she breathed out slowly, lost in the deep green of his gaze.

'Then, thank you.' Her heart felt suddenly light and gauzy, as though it might fly away at any moment. 'That doesn't seem like nearly enough. But I don't know what else to say.'

Rollo stared at her in silence.

Since leaving Daisy at the spa he hadn't been able to stop thinking about her. Or, more precisely, about having sex with her. And now that they were finally alone, it felt like the best idea he'd ever had. Not only would it create an intimacy that might conceivably add credibility to their 'relationship,' but it would also solve the aching physical frustration that had plagued him since he'd kissed her in his office nearly two weeks ago.

It was true she shared many of his mother's flaws, only there was one crucial difference. Alice Fleming's power had lain in her emotional hold over him. She'd been his mother and he had loved her. But he didn't love Daisy. So where was the risk?

The air seemed to swell around them.

Slowly he reached out and cupped her chin with his hand. 'Then don't say anything,' he murmured.

Her whole body was trembling, bones melting,

blood beating inside her like a warning drum. Only then his eyes focused hungrily on her mouth and suddenly nothing mattered except the gathering storm rising inside her.

Standing up on her toes, she ran her tongue slowly across his lips.

He tasted of champagne and ice.

And danger.

Delicious. Intoxicating. It was the perfect cocktail.

Her head was swimming and she took a soft, swift breath like a gasp, her hands fluttering against his shirt.

'Kiss me,' she said hoarsely. 'Kiss me now.'

Rollo stared at her, his body in turmoil, the beat of his blood slowing to a pulsing adagio. Her eyes were shimmering; her face was soft and still and utterly irresistible.

He had no choice and, leaning forward, he kissed her fiercely. Instantly he was lost in the heat and softness of her lips, and as her fingers curled round his arms—gripping, tugging, tearing at his shirt— he felt his body harden with such speed and intensity that he almost blacked out.

'Daisy, wait—'

Lifting his mouth from hers, trying to slow down

the pace, he groaned against her lips, his face taut with concentration.

'Slow down, sweetheart—' He was fighting to get his words out. 'Or I won't be able to hold on until we get upstairs.'

He felt her body tense against him, and a flicker of apprehension, bright and jagged like lightning, cut through the dark clouds of passion fogging his brain.

'Why do we need to go upstairs?'

He breathed out unsteadily. 'I just thought it would be more private.'

The word, with its whispered hints of closed doors and darkened bedrooms, scraped over his skin and suddenly he didn't care where they were. Staring down into her face, he only cared about the warmth and the sweetness of her body against his.

'But we can do whatever you want,' he said hoarsely. 'Wherever you want…'

CHAPTER SIX

'*WHATEVER YOU WANT...wherever you want...*'

Daisy felt her body still, her mind snagging on an image of Rollo pulling off his shirt, his green eyes softening as he drew her closer to the hard contours of his chest—

The floor tilted and it was as though she was free-falling. The rush of desire and longing was so intense that she could hardly stand.

She wanted him.

But even as she acknowledged the truth of that statement she felt the sharp tug of the parachute pulling her back.

But what would happen if she gave in to that craving?

'No.' Stumbling backwards, she shook her head, her heart beating faster. 'We can't. We shouldn't. It's not right.'

Rollo stared at her in silence, the sudden distance in her voice jarring his senses. What was she talking about? *Can't. Shouldn't. Not right.*

His confusion hardened into irritation. 'I fail to see why,' he said slowly. 'We're both adults who want to have sex.'

Daisy flinched, but held his gaze. He was right. On both counts. But evidently two rights made a wrong, for—whatever her body might be telling her to the contrary—she knew it would be a disaster if they ended up in bed together. And Rollo knew it as well as she did. He just didn't like being told so.

She pushed against his chest. 'That may be reason enough for you. But there's a little more to it for me than just lust and being over the age of consent.'

'Like what? Love and romance?'

The sudden chill in his eyes as much as the harshness in his voice made her breath stutter in her throat.

'I'm a businessman—not a fourteen-year-old girl. We *are* getting married though. Won't that do?'

She jerked her hands away, the pulse at the base of her neck beating wildly. She could feel his hostility, see it in the set of his shoulders, but she didn't care. Nothing mattered except wiping that sneer off his irritatingly handsome face.

'It might have done *if* I wanted to have sex with you. But I don't.'

He shook his head, his lip curling into a sneer. 'So you're *still* a liar. Only now you're a tease, as well!'

Her fingernails cut into the palms of her hands. 'And you're back to calling me names.'

His eyes narrowed. 'I'll stop calling you names when you stop deserving them. I think that's fair, don't you?'

She felt anger—dark and fast—swirl and rush over her like floodwater. It was true, she had wanted him in the heat of the moment—she still did, judging by the pulsing ache in her pelvis. But his conceited assumption that she would fall at his feet, or rather into his bed, rankled with her.

'I don't care what you think.' She glowered at him. 'It was only a kiss. And just because I kiss a man it doesn't mean I automatically want to have sex with him.' Her hands curled into small, tight fists. 'Especially when the only reason I'm kissing him is for my job.'

He didn't reply at once—just stared at her in silence, his face cold and set like a bronze mask.

'Your job!' His derisive smile stung her skin. 'So that was a spot of overtime, was it?'

'No. That was a mistake!'

Her whole body trembled with fury. For a moment she couldn't speak. She was too busy hating him and his snide remarks.

'I thought you understood it was fake—just like we're faking the rest of this relationship.' She glared at him. 'But, of course, I completely forgot about your overinflated ego.'

Throwing her hands up in exasperation, she turned and walked swiftly towards the kitchen.

Rollo stared after her in silence, anger rolling beneath his skin like molten lava.

She was lying to his face. He didn't care how much she claimed otherwise. He'd felt her respond. He knew that kiss had been real.

More than real.

It had been hot and raw and urgent.

Only now she was trying to twist the facts—pretending *he'd* misinterpreted *her* behaviour and that *he* was the unreasonable one.

His mouth thinned. Daisy was more like his mother than he could ever have imagined. Honesty hadn't come naturally to Alice Fleming either. Instead she too had leapfrogged from story to story, lashing out with accusations when cornered.

Heart pounding, he stalked angrily across the living room into the kitchen.

Glancing over to where she stood, he felt his chest grow hot and tight. Above the disdainful curve of that temptingly soft pink mouth, her dark brown eyes shimmered beneath the lights. Another man might have lost his way in the perfection of that face. But, growing up with his restless, manipulative mother, he'd learnt early that beauty was only skin-deep.

'You need to worry less about the size of my ego and more about the gaps in your memory,' he snarled.

Daisy turned to face him. 'What are you talking about?'

'We had an agreement—*have* an agreement—about honesty.'

Honesty! Looking into his eyes, she saw the simmering fury, the thwarted authority, and felt her body start to shake. This wasn't about honesty. It was about pride. His stupid male pride.

Squaring her shoulders, she leaned against the worktop and scowled. '*You're* the one with a faulty memory, Rollo. I told you our relationship wouldn't include sex.'

His eyes blazed. 'And yet you asked me to kiss you.' His voice rose. '*You* asked *me* to kiss you!'

He swore beneath his breath, his eyes fierce with passion.

'Why are you being like this? I know you want me, Daisy. And I want you. Like I've never wanted any woman—ever. I can't sleep. I can't work. It's driving me crazy—'

As he broke off Daisy felt a treacherous warmth slide over her skin, the pull of his words strong and relentless like a riptide. And then abruptly she shivered. *Of course he wanted her.* She'd rejected him. Men like Rollo didn't like to be thwarted.

'You want me because you can't have me,' she said flatly. 'That's all.'

There was a long, gritty silence.

Finally he drew in a breath. 'That doesn't explain why you kissed me.'

She couldn't speak—didn't want to reply. But he waited and waited, and she knew from the uncompromising set of his jaw that he was going to keep on waiting until she gave him an answer.

Not just an answer but the truth.

Looking down, she swallowed. 'I kissed you because for one utterly senseless moment, part of me—the stupid, weak, irrational part I despise—wanted to have sex with you,' she said at last.

There was a fraction of a pause, then he said quietly, 'What about the rest?'

She frowned. 'The rest?'

Glancing up, she felt her pulse stumble. She'd supposed he would be gloating, but there was no sign of triumph. Instead his jaw was taut and his eyes were searching her face.

'You know—the smart, strong, rational part you admire.'

With shock, she realised he was attempting to make a joke. But she didn't laugh. She couldn't even smile. She felt too exposed, too vulnerable.

Shrugging, she stared past him. 'Our relationship is complicated enough, Rollo. Sex would just make it even more muddled.'

His eyes on her face were clear and unflinching. 'I disagree. Sex is simple. It's people who make it complicated. They expect too much. But you and I, we don't have to worry about that.'

She stared over at him, dry-mouthed, recognising the truth in his words. For she'd done it herself—confused sex with intimacy and love, and been left feeling foolish and crushed. And he was right: that wouldn't happen with them. There wouldn't be any expectations or disappointment or pain.

'Do you know how rare that is, Daisy? We can't let this moment pass.'

His face was expressionless, but something in his voice made her body twitch in response.

It would just be sex.

Pure, primal passion.

As though reading her thoughts, his eyes rested on her face.

'I know you feel it,' he said softly. 'I feel it too… because I want what you want.'

She shivered, tasting his words in her mouth.

'What do you want?'

Her voice was hoarse, her breath burning inside her chest as hesitantly he reached out and touched her throat, resting his hand softly against her pulse, so that her heart began to beat hard and slow.

'I want this…'

He lifted his fingers and pressed them lightly against her mouth.

'And this.'

Breathing out unsteadily, he stepped closer. With fingers that were both gentle and firm he loosened her ponytail, catching hold of the long, blonde hair. For one infinitesimal moment they stared at one another in silence. And then heat rushed through her as he tugged her head back, his pupils flaring.

'And this.'

He brought his mouth down hard on hers, his hand tightening in her hair, fingers grasping her scalp. Pulse racing, blood thickening, she leaned into him, her body melting against his as he deepened the kiss. She felt dizzy, desperate, her mind devoid of anything but the firmness of his lips and the need to feel him—his body, his skin.

She ran her hands over his shirt, her eyes widening as he pushed her fingers aside and undid the buttons, peeling the crisp fabric slowly away from his skin. She stared at him in silence. He was so beautiful...so golden and smooth and flawless. Gently, hesitantly, she touched his stomach, tracing the definition of muscle with her finger.

Instantly he sucked in a breath and, looking up, she saw that his face was stiff with concentration, his body taut, muscles tense.

'Are you sure?'

His voice was thick and constricted. She could hear the effort it was taking him to pause, to ask the question.

'I want you to be sure.'

Daisy stared at him dazedly, her pulse fluttering, her whole body vibrating with heat and need and emotion.

'I am. I'm sure. I want this.' She swallowed, the ache inside her throbbing in time to her heartbeat. 'I want you.'

His face was still, his eyes dark pinpoints.

'And I want you too.'

Reaching out, he slid his hands gently over her collarbone and shoulders, pushing the straps of her dress down so that suddenly she was shivering, the cold air shocking her skin.

Rollo felt his groin tighten, hot tension flowering inside him.

She was wearing no bra.

He stared at her in silence, his gaze blunted by her beauty.

Then, wordlessly, he cupped her breasts in his hand, thumbs grazing the nipples. Slowly he bent his head and licked the tips, the blood beating wildly inside his chest as he felt them harden beneath his tongue, heard her soft moan. Then, lifting his mouth, he found her lips and, easing them open, he deepened the kiss, his hands pushing the dress down over her hips, the silken fabric brushing over his fingers as it slipped to the floor.

Daisy shuddered. His mouth was on her face, her

throat, her collarbone, ceaseless and insistent. His fingers were sliding over her skin, sending shivers of heat in every direction, touching every nerve so that she moved restlessly against him.

'Rollo...'

She could hear the longing, the pleading in her own voice, but she didn't care. Nothing mattered except his touch.

Only she wanted more...

She needed more.

Looping her arm around his neck, she pressed against him, sweetness spreading inside her as she felt his body rise and swell. She was tugging at his belt, the button, the zip, her blood beating inside her.

With a rough groan, Rollo pulled back. His heart was pounding, his body groaning in protest. He wanted Daisy with an intensity that he'd never felt for any woman. But he also wanted to demonstrate his power over her.

And over himself.

He needed to prove that he would never surrender to any woman—not even, perhaps especially not, to one as beautiful and seductive as Daisy.

His heart thumped, his mouth seeking hers again as he lifted her onto the worktop. Pulling her legs apart, he gently pushed aside the flimsy fabric of her panties, his breath stilling in his throat as she melted against his fingertips, her thighs clenching around his hand.

'Let it go,' he whispered against her mouth.

Daisy shuddered. Her whole body was dissolving beneath the teasing torment of his fingers. But it was not enough. Not enough to purge her body of the relentless aching tightness inside her. And, raising her hips, she rocked against him, a quivering pulse spilling over her hot, damp skin.

'Don't stop,' she gasped. 'Don't stop—'

And then her muscles tensed and she was arching upwards, shuddering, unravelling, her hands grasping at his arms, her mind blank of everything but the heat and the hardness of his hand cupping her body...

Glancing down at the sweet vintage-style dress she was wearing, Daisy frowned. Was it too flippant for a 'philanthropic benefit luncheon'? Possibly. But there was no time to change. The limousine would be arriving soon and they couldn't be late. Rollo was one of the guest speakers.

Rollo.

Her muscles clenched, and suddenly she felt as

though she were suffocating. Just thinking his name gave her a head rush. But clearly Rollo didn't feel the same way for despite what had happened in the kitchen, he seemed in no rush whatsoever to consummate their relationship.

She bit her lip. In fact, the only hint of the passionate moment they'd shared had been later as they made their way towards their respective bedrooms when he'd hesitated, then pulled her against him, kissing her fiercely as if he couldn't help himself.

Lying alone in her bed, her body hot and twitching beneath the cool sheets, she had finally fallen asleep, her mind aching and exhausted with trying to make sense of his behaviour.

Waking, she had hoped they could talk. But, having both overslept, there had been no time to chat or enjoy a leisurely breakfast. Instead he'd been polite but strangely detached, given how intimate and uninhibited they had been just hours earlier. Remembering just how uninhibited she had been, Daisy felt her cheeks grow hot.

It was all very confusing, and more than a little embarrassing.

Glancing at her reflection, she breathed out slowly. She'd think about it later. Right now she had a job to do, and with one last twirl she turned and walked back into the bedroom.

'You look nice.'

Her breath jammed in her throat, her eyes widening with shock. Rollo was standing in the doorway to her room, watching her calmly. As usual his expression was utterly indecipherable. He might have just been elected mayor of New York, or just as easily have lost all his money on the stock market. It was impossible to tell.

She stared at him accusingly. 'You scared me.'

'Sorry. I did knock.'

'I didn't hear you,' she said quickly. 'I was just changing my shoes. I thought I'd wear heels.'

'I like them.' His eyes dropped to the black patent court heels and then roamed lazily over her dress. 'I like all of it. You look beautiful.'

Her face grew hot and tight, and she was suddenly unbearably conscious of her body's response to his precision-cut attention.

'Good. That's great,' she said mechanically and, picking up her phone, she glanced pointedly at the screen. 'We should go. Otherwise we'll be late.'

But he didn't move. Instead he shifted against the door frame, his green eyes fixed on her face.

'Actually, we won't. I cancelled.'

It was a first. The first time he'd ever put his private life before work. And certainly the first time a woman had been at the top of his agenda.

What made his behaviour as baffling as it was unsettling was that he hadn't even planned on doing it. It had just happened.

Sitting at his desk, he'd truly believed he would be attending the luncheon—right up to the moment when his subconscious had overridden his conscious brain and he'd picked up the phone and told his assistant to make his apologies.

But, planned or not, it was clear from his uncharacteristic behaviour that, despite his trying to treat his relationship with Daisy like any other business arrangement, she had brought chaos to his world. And now his life was full of precedents.

Including this self-inflicted discomfort in his groin.

Theoretically, last night had seemed like the perfect opportunity to demonstrate to Daisy that *he* was the one pulling the strings. Now, though, he could see that his logic might have been flawed. Not only was his body aching with frustration, but the satisfaction he'd felt at having made his point had been pretty much eclipsed by confusion

over what it was he'd actually proved to Daisy—
or himself.

Glancing up, he found her watching him warily.

'You don't seem very pleased,' he remarked.

Her eyes darted past him. 'I thought you were
giving a speech?'

He shrugged. 'I was. But there are always far too
many speakers at those lunches. Besides...'

He lengthened the word so that it pressed against
her skin like a cold knife.

'I'd rather just speak to you.'

Her heart gave a thump.

'Okay.'

A cold feeling was settling in the pit of her stomach and her eyes focused longingly on the door.

'I thought we weren't going to fight any more.'

Hearing the hesitation in her voice, he frowned.
'Talking doesn't have to mean fighting.'

Except that up to now it had.

He felt a stab of frustration. But why was he trying to coax her anyway? He should just *tell* her she
was having lunch with him. Only suddenly—incredibly—he found himself wanting it to be her
choice. For some inexplicable reason that seemed
more important than getting his own way.

He held her gaze. 'Have lunch with me. Please. I promise we won't fight. I just want to talk.'

Daisy stared at him. He looked serious and sincere. And very handsome. Feeling the knot of tension inside her loosen a fraction, she nodded slowly.

'I'd like that very much.'

Twenty minutes later the limousine pulled up outside a small restaurant with a flaking green-painted facade somewhere in East Harlem.

Glancing up at the name above the door, Daisy felt her body stiffen with shock. She'd heard of Bova's, but she'd never imagined eating there. Surely this couldn't be it? It was supposed to be the most exclusive restaurant in New York, but this place looked as though it might close down before they finished their meal.

She bit her lip. 'Is this that restaurant where even celebrities can't get a table?'

He hesitated, as though he was making some kind of decision. Then finally he nodded slowly. 'It is. But I happen to know the owner.' He held out his hand. 'Come on. Let's eat.'

Inside, the restaurant was even smaller than it had looked from the street. There were only seven tables, and all of them bar one were full.

'I hope you like Italian,' Rollo said as they sat down. 'Other than pizza, I mean.'

His mouth curved and, looking up, she saw his eyes were light and teasing, and a ripple of happiness went through her like an electric current.

She smiled. 'I love it,' she said truthfully. 'Especially the desserts.'

He seemed pleased.

'Then you must have the cannoli. It's sublime.' He frowned. 'I should have said—they don't have a menu here. If you're a regular, they know what you like and they cook it for you.'

Lifting his head, he paused as a waiter approached the table, and she felt a prickle of awe and envy as he switched into rapid and clearly fluent Italian.

Turning back to face her, he frowned. 'I hope you don't mind, but I took the liberty of ordering for you. I wouldn't know where to start with most people, but you're different. I know you as well as I know myself.'

His eyes on hers were very green.

Daisy blinked. 'Really?'

'Well, I should. That's the reason we've spent so much time getting our stories straight.'

He gave her a quick, dazzling smile and she nodded mechanically. Had she really imagined that he thought she was special in some way? Heart banging in her throat, she picked up her glass, hoping to hide her confusion.

'I'm sure it'll be delicious.'

Her heart was still pounding in her chest and, desperate to disguise the effect of his words, she gave him what she hoped was a cool smile.

'I'm actually really excited. I don't eat out much. I never have. I think it's probably because of working so much at the diner with Mum and Dad.'

His eyes gleamed. 'Don't knock the Love Shack.'

She screwed up her face. 'I'm not. It's great— and they're great. And they love what they do, and they love each other, and that's why it's the Love Shack.'

She stopped abruptly. Her voice was too high and forced. But right now was not a good time to discuss her parents—particularly their *perfect* marriage. Not when she was sitting opposite her soon-to-be fake husband.

Desperate to change the subject, she glanced round the restaurant. 'It's not what I expected.' She frowned. 'It's so small and…'

'Ordinary?' he suggested. His expression was

unreadable but his eyes were watching her carefully.

She nodded. 'It feels like someone's dining room.' Her eyes flickered over the faces of the other diners, widening as they stopped on a dark-haired man wearing a polo shirt.

'Isn't that…?'

Rollo held his finger up to his lips. 'It is. And that is his equally famous wife. They live in Tribeca. They come here twice a month.'

'They do?'

Hearing her surprise, he shrugged. 'The food here is the best in the city.'

She nodded, her pulse quickening. She believed him. But for the last few days, her life had been spent learning his life, and she knew that there was something more beneath his words. She could feel it in the way he rearranged his glass, hear it in the hair-fine tension in his voice.

'So, do you come here regularly too?'

He nodded. 'Probably a couple of times a week most weeks.'

As the waiter returned, bringing olives and water, Daisy stared down at her cutlery, his words scraping against her skin like fingernails on a blackboard. A couple of times *a week*! How many women was that a year?

She frowned, feeling some of her happiness oozing away.

But why was she counting? Rollo's private life was none of her business. She didn't have to care about his past. Or worry about being the latest in an ever-growing line of women that he brought to the same restaurant.

That was the upside to this whole crazy situation, and the beauty of their relationship. She could stay detached, unemotional, immune.

Or that was what was supposed to happen.

She caught her breath, shocked to discover that wasn't how she was feeling at all. Instead a thin curl of misery was coiling around her brain.

'You're very quiet.'

Rollo's voice bumped into her thoughts.

'I was just thinking.' She gave him a small, tight smile. 'Trying to work something out. A sum.'

He stared at her in a way that made her heart skid forward.

'A sum! You're not going to suggest we go halves on the bill, are you?'

'No! Although I don't see why I shouldn't. I'm

not Orphan Annie, you know. I do have some money.'

He ignored her. 'So, what are you trying to work out?'

'It doesn't matter.' Her voice sounded more desperate than she'd intended and, picking up her glass, she took a sip of water. 'Truly. It was nothing.'

There was a brief silence. His eyes were level with hers and she forced herself to keep looking at him as he gazed at her thoughtfully.

'Okay,' he said after a moment. 'But promise me that if whatever it is becomes a problem, even if it's not really your problem, you'll tell me. So I can help.'

It was Daisy's turn to stay silent. He thought she was worrying about David's debt, and it had sounded almost as if he cared. As if he actually wanted to help.

The blood was humming in her ears and her heart was suddenly beating too fast and too loud. She glanced across at him, her eyes scanning his face. But had he meant it? Or was he just being in character? Saying what a doting boyfriend would say to the woman he loved?

She looked up at him with a smile that betrayed none of her confusion. 'Okay. I promise.'

'Good. I've ordered a Chianti with our food. Is that okay?'

She blinked, caught off guard by the change of subject and by the sudden realisation that they were talking normally—almost like they were a real couple.

'Of course.'

'They do an excellent Montespertoli here.'

'I'll take your word for it. I don't really know much about wine. David buys it and I just drink it.'

He grinned. 'I have much the same arrangement with my sommelier.'

'You have your own sommelier?'

'Of course,' he said, feigning astonishment. 'Doesn't everyone?'

She laughed. 'Of course! In fact, I need to check in with mine—make sure he approves of your choice.'

His eyes were glittering. 'Trust me, I've made the right choice.'

She felt her breath explode inside her chest. Obviously he was talking about the wine or the food or maybe both. But her head was spinning, her heart speeding like a getaway car, and she knew that more than anything she wanted him to be talking about *her*.

When finally she felt that she could trust her voice, she tilted her head and said, 'So, how do you know it's the right wine?'

'Wine? Is that what we're talking about?'

His eyes rested on her face and she felt her colour rise. But, holding his gaze, she nodded.

'Come on. I really want to know. I promise not to tell my sommelier if you don't tell yours.'

Laughing softly, he leaned forward over the table, so that suddenly she was conscious of the solidity of his shoulders and the symmetry of his face.

'Okay… Well, if, say, the food has lots of flavour it would need to be partnered with something rich and smooth and sexy—'

She swallowed; her mouth felt suddenly dry, her throat like sandpaper. He might have been talking about himself. She felt an ache, sharp and intense like hunger. Only she knew it wasn't the sort of hunger that could be satisfied by food.

'Basically, you just need to trust your instincts.' Pausing, he glanced over her shoulder. 'Ah, excellent. I'm starving.'

Watching the waiters put their plates on the table, Daisy felt her appetite return.

As Rollo had promised, the meal was delicious. Tiny baby clams stuffed with breadcrumbs to start, followed by ravioli with pear and ricotta. The main course was osso buco—veal shanks in white wine and lemon.

Pressing her napkin against her lips, Daisy laid her knife and fork down on her empty plate. 'That was perfect.'

'I'm glad you liked it.'

His eyes across the table gave nothing away and, taking a deep breath, she said carefully, 'I can see why you bring all your dates here.'

He didn't answer. Around them, the air seemed to grow thicker, and she felt a nervous shudder run down her spine.

'I don't bring *all* my dates here,' he said quietly. 'In fact, you're the first *date* I've ever brought here.'

Daisy felt her heart punch against her chest.

'But you said you come twice a week, most weeks.'

'And I do. On my own.'

She swallowed. Men like Rollo didn't dine alone.

'I don't understand.'

He shrugged. His face looked shuttered, remote.

'It's like a home to me. I've been coming here ever since I was thirteen. The owner, Joe, his father, Vinnie, gave me my first job.'

He smiled—only it was a smile that made something inside her shift and crack open.

'What did you do?' she said hoarsely.

'I washed dishes at first. Then I was a waiter. *Just* a waiter,' he amended, his eyes meeting hers. 'They wouldn't trust me in the kitchen.'

She nodded. 'Very wise.' She tried a smile of her own. 'I've seen you incinerating toast. I definitely wouldn't trust you with veal.'

He smiled again, but this time it touched his eyes and she felt a rush of happiness and surprise—for when had she started wanting to make him happy?

'Would you like that cannoli?' He was back in control, his hand half-raised towards the waiter.

Groaning, she shook her head. 'Yes. But I can't. I would love a coffee though.'

The coffee arrived, together with a small dark green box.

Daisy made a face. 'Are those chocolates?'

He nodded. 'But they're very small. Go on.' Smiling a little, he pushed the box towards her. 'Have one, otherwise I'll never hear the end of it.'

Sighing, she picked it up and pulled off the lid. 'They'd better be small,' she grumbled, 'otherwise you'll never...'

Her voice trailed off.

It wasn't chocolates. Instead, nestling on top of pale green paper was a beautiful diamond-and-emerald ring.

She stared at it—stunned, mesmerised.

'I hope you don't mind. I asked Joe to help out.'

He gestured to where a large dark-haired man stood beaming.

She looked up, groping for the right words—any words, in fact. But her mind seemed to have stopped functioning.

'Yes—I mean, no...I don't mind,' she managed finally. 'Oh, Rollo, it's beautiful. I love it.'

'Here. Let me.'

She watched him slip the ring onto her finger, his hands warm and solid against hers.

'So, will you marry me?'

His voice was soft. For a split second she forgot it wasn't real. Forgot it was all just part of their performance. Then slowly, she nodded. 'Yes, I will.' She hesitated. 'But why here? Why now?'

He shrugged. 'Why wait? I want everyone to know that you're going to be my wife.'

He hadn't planned on giving her the ring until later. But last night everything had changed. Finally she'd been honest with him, admitting her desire in the most blatant of terms. Saying that she wanted sex, that she wanted him.

It had been like a starter pistol going off in his head.

Suddenly proposing had seemed like the obvious next step. And with Daisy wearing his ring their 'marriage' was a step closer to being real—a step closer to the moment when James Dunmore would finally sell to him.

Back in the limousine, Daisy couldn't stop looking at her finger.

'Relax. It's not going anywhere.'

She looked up. Rollo was watching her meditatively.

'I know. I just like looking at it.' Holding out her hand, she twisted the ring from side to side. If being seen with Rollo in public had been like putting on a parachute, this was like jumping out of the plane. Now it really was real. She was his fiancée.

'I suppose I should tell my parents and David.'

'I suppose so.' His eyebrows raised mockingly.

'But let's just have a couple of hours to get used to it ourselves.'

The next moment an electric thrill snaked over her skin as his fingertips brushed against hers.

'If it needs to be altered, tell me.'

She nodded. 'I will. I don't want it falling off.'

'Neither do I. It's got to go back to the jewellers in a year.'

Staring fixedly at the ring, Daisy felt her stomach plummet like a broken kite.

A moment ago she'd felt like Cinderella. Now though, she realised she was actually Sleeping Beauty—only the Prince hadn't woken her with a kiss. He'd tipped her out of bed and onto the floor.

Her head was pounding.

So what if he had? She knew it wasn't a real proposal. They weren't in love; their entire relationship was a sham. They were only together to convince Dunmore to sell his building to Rollo.

But for some reason none of that seemed to matter right now. She still felt like a failure. Just as she had when Nick had broken up with her. And before him, Jamie.

She'd thought they'd loved each other. She'd been wrong. And they'd been wrong for her. Only it had still been devastating to accept—particularly when all she really wanted was that effortless understanding with someone that her parents shared.

But it was supposed to be different with Rollo. With him she had thought she could relax and not worry about getting hurt.

Her heart twisted.

Except that apparently she'd got that wrong too.

Slowly she withdrew her hand and pressed it against her forehead.

'What's the matter?'

'Nothing. Just a headache. I expect it's drinking wine at lunchtime. I probably just need to have a lie-down.'

Rollo stared at her in silence. *A headache?*

Angrily, he looked down at the ring on her finger, its glittering facets like so many mocking faces. Back at the restaurant it had felt so real. The food, the conversation… He'd even told her about working there—something he'd never shared with anyone. But now she was lying to him. *Again*, he thought, with an almost unbearable sting of swift, startled astonishment.

'Perhaps you could just tell the truth.' Shaking his head, he stared down into her wide, shocked eyes. 'That you're upset about having to return the ring. Surely you didn't think you were going to *keep* it?'

For a moment she was too shocked to speak. Then slowly she felt a shivering hot anger slide over her skin.

'Yes, I did. And I thought you would give me half the apartment too,' she said curtly. 'No, Rollo, of course I didn't think that. I hadn't even thought about a ring at all until you gave me this one. Why would I? You said you were going to go public with the engagement in a couple of months.'

His lip curled. 'So I changed my mind? I thought women liked spontaneity.'

She glared at him. 'And I'm just a woman? How romantic!'

He stared at her in exasperation. 'It's not meant to be romantic. This is a business arrangement.'

'Fine! Then I don't need this. Here!'

Reaching down, she tugged the ring off her finger and held it out to him.

He ignored her hand, his face hardening. She was impossible. Irrational. Ungrateful. He could have thrown her and her brother to the wolves, but instead he'd given her a second chance, just like his father.

Leaning forward, he thumped on the window behind the chauffeur's head.

'What are you doing?' Daisy was looking at him, her eyes wide with shock.

'I'm getting out. I need some fresh air.'

'But you can't just walk away. We need to talk.'

Her anger was giving way to confusion and fear.

But as the car slid smoothly to a halt he yanked open the door, an expression on his face that she couldn't decipher.

'There's no point,' he said flatly. 'I really don't think we have anything more to say to one another.' And then, before she had a chance to reply, he was on the pavement, vanishing into the crowds as the car started to move forward again.

CHAPTER SEVEN

BACK AT THE APARTMENT, Daisy stared blankly around the living room, the tears she'd managed to hold back in the limousine burning her eyes.

What had he meant by nothing left to say?

But, recalling the flat finality of his tone, she felt her chest tighten and she knew what he'd meant.

He meant it was over.

And now her brother was going to pay the price.

Her mind began to race; her breath came fast and jerky, as though she'd been running.

She needed to warn David. She needed to be the one to tell him about the deal she'd made and wrecked. Her stomach shrank. And about what would happen next...

Panic crawled over her skin and, heart pounding, she walked dazedly upstairs. She would pack and then she would leave.

But if she left, there would be no going back. Shouldn't she at least try and talk to Rollo again?

But as she pictured his cool, expressionless face,

her hands began to shake, and abruptly she sat down on the bed.

Rollo couldn't have made it clearer that he had nothing to say to her.

She lifted her chin, felt her heartbeat steadying. Then she would just have to do the talking—even if it was only to say goodbye.

He might be about to unleash hell, but she wasn't a coward. And, although she knew she'd made mistakes, she wasn't going to make herself look guiltier than she was by running away.

If only her hands would stop shaking.

Glancing down to where they lay in her lap, she caught sight of the ring and, stomach cramping, she slowly pulled it off her finger and laid it on the bedside table. She didn't need it anymore and, whatever Rollo might think, she didn't want it either. Even looking at it made her feel sick and helpless.

But staying to face him was her choice. And that meant she *wasn't* helpless, and whatever happened next, she needed to remember that. Now though, it was time to pack. Not because she expected him back anytime soon—it was, after all, a working day—but because she simply couldn't sit and wait for him. She needed to do something.

Heart heaving, she found her suitcase and began to fill it, barely registering what she was putting in, her arms and hands acting by themselves. Finally it was done. But as she fumbled with the zip, the air seemed to ripple around her and there was a sudden shift in the light. Looking up, she felt her throat close over tightly.

Rollo was blocking the doorway. The same doorway where he'd stood just a few hours earlier, when she'd tried to read his mood. Only this time she didn't need to try. His mood was unmistakable. He was utterly, shatteringly furious.

'Y-you're back,' she stammered, her stomach plummeting beneath his blank-eyed hostility. 'I wasn't expecting you.'

Rollo gritted his teeth, his gaze shifting from her face to the suitcase lying on the bed, and suddenly his whole body tightened and he was breathing too fast.

Packing her bags had been one of his mother's favourite tricks too.

Only for show though. He knew that because when she finally had left for real she'd taken no suitcase. She hadn't needed one. Of course she'd taken what mattered. But she'd left everything else behind.

Including her son.

And the note justifying her actions.

He felt sick. Anger and pain sliced through him but, pushing down his nausea, he met Daisy's gaze, his eyes narrowing with contempt.

'Clearly.'

'I didn't mean—'

'Save it. I know what you meant. And even if I didn't, the suitcase is a bit of a giveaway.'

'I—I wasn't running away. I was waiting. For you.'

'Of course.' His lip curled into a sneer. 'You're an actress. Your USP is making an entrance and an exit. But it works best with an audience.'

Rage was pounding inside his head.

He'd actually started to think she might be different. That maybe he'd misjudged her. Only he'd been wrong. Not just wrong, but obtuse. Forgetting all the lessons he'd learned from childhood, he'd let himself be fooled by Daisy's beauty and sexual allure.

Only he wasn't a little boy any more. He was a man—the owner of a global property company worth billions, who'd worked hard to build his business. Harder still to keep his life free of the sort of emotional tension and uncertainty he hated.

Which was why he'd brought their engagement forward.

It had been a unilateral decision, and as such a clear reminder to Daisy that *he* was in charge. And, of course, the first solid proof he could give Dunmore that he was a changed man—a man in love and committed to one woman.

Deep down though, what really mattered—what he had needed to know, to see and feel for himself—was that Daisy could be open and honest. When she'd finally not only admitted her desire but responded so feverishly to his touch it had been the assurance he'd needed to accelerate their relationship.

Only watching her open the ring box, he'd found himself in the extraordinary position of feeling nervous about how she would react. Worse, in the limousine she'd lied *again*, and he'd felt the same shifting unease, the same devastating, unbearable insecurity that had blighted his childhood.

And now she'd packed her bags.

His gaze shifted to her face, eyes hardening.

'I'd like to say I'm surprised or disappointed. But, given your character, it's all quite tragically predictable.'

Daisy flinched inwardly at his words but she

forced her eyes up to meet his. 'You can insult me all you like. I don't care. I only stayed to tell you that I'm going to see David, so if you could—'

He cut across her.

'How thoughtful. The caring sister. He *will* be pleased.'

Meeting his cool, expressionless gaze, she felt misery clutch low at her stomach. So this was how it was going to be. He was going to play with her, punish her as he'd wanted to do right from the start—before he'd decided she was more use to him as a 'wife.'

'I know you're angry, Rollo, but this isn't all about you. Or us.'

He shook his head, fury spiralling inside him, his heartbeat slamming into his ribs. Had what happened last night and in the restaurant really affected her so little?

He gritted his teeth. The answer to that question was packed and ready to go.

'But, let me guess, it is about you.' His voice was rising. 'And your brother.'

She breathed out unsteadily, trying to ignore his contempt and animosity.

'It was only ever about David, and you knew

that. Look, I can't stop you calling the police. But I want to be there with him when they turn up.'

He gave a humourless laugh.

'You really are a drama queen, aren't you?' He gestured towards her suitcase. 'And how you love your props.'

'It's not a prop,' she snapped, a flicker of anger catching fire inside her. 'How else I am supposed to pack my things?'

'You don't need to pack. This is all just for show. Like everything else you do.'

Her head jerked up, eyes darkening with outrage.

'Like everything we both do, you mean. You are such a hypocrite. Our entire relationship is a soap opera of *your* making, and you've got the nerve to accuse *me* of being a drama queen.'

'This is not my idea of a relationship,' he snarled.

'Well, it certainly isn't mine.' She bit the words out between her teeth. 'It's more like living in a war zone.'

'Then maybe you should stop turning everything into a fight.'

'Me! What about you? You're the one who threw a tantrum in the middle of Madison Avenue, storming off like some three-year-old.'

It was true. He had behaved childishly. But it was

her fault. He might have a reputation as an ice-cold negotiator, but with Daisy his temper hovered between volatile and volcanic. It was an admission that did nothing to defuse his anger with her—or himself. In fact, it just seemed to wind him up more tightly than ever.

He stared at her coldly.

'Oh but you throwing the ring I gave you back in my face—that was just so mature.'

'I wasn't trying to be mature,' she snapped. 'I was upset.'

'You weren't upset. You were gutted. As soon as you saw the ring you thought you were going to get to keep it.'

He saw the sudden startled flinch in her eyes but ignored it. 'And when you found out that wasn't going to happen *you* had a tantrum—'

'That's not true! Or fair. I hadn't even thought about you giving me a ring.'

It was true—she hadn't. At least she hadn't thought about him doing so with such sensitivity. She'd supposed there would be a ring, but that it would be just a ring.

Remembering the effort he'd made in the restaurant to surprise her, she felt her eyes grow hot. 'How can you accuse me of plotting to keep it?'

He could hear the shake in her voice, and knew he'd hurt her. Knew too, that he was being unfair, unreasonable, cruel. But he wasn't about to start indulging Daisy the way his father had indulged his mother.

It was why he'd arranged this relationship with her in the first place—precisely to avoid that kind of emotional manipulation.

'I find that hard to believe. You could hardly take your eyes off it in the car.'

Fighting tears, Daisy shook her head. Did he really think so little of her? Had it not occurred to him that she might have another, innocent, less self-serving motive for admiring the ring?

'Not because I thought it was mine—'

Suddenly she couldn't speak. How could she explain it to Rollo? A man who was indifferent, brutally dismissive of anything romantic. A man who dealt solely in facts. Who reduced everything to assets and liabilities. A man who was happy to fake his own marriage solely to con a business rival.

How could she expect him to understand that she hadn't been acting?

That just for a moment, when he'd slid the ring onto her finger, everything had felt real and perfect. Just like she'd imagined it would in her fantasies of love.

Her eyes blurred.

Only, of course, it was just as phony as the rest of their relationship. What was more, it had been nothing to do with *her*.

Her heartbeat froze and, remembering how she had squirmed beneath his fingers, her body opening up to his, she felt suddenly sick.

No wonder he had been able to hold himself back. That had all been just an act too. Another way to demonstrate his power over her. Only that time he'd used her greedy body, not her brother, to prove the point.

'Think what you want.' She breathed out shakily. 'I don't care.' Reaching down, she picked up the suitcase. 'Like you said earlier, we have nothing more to say to each other, so if you don't mind, I'm going to see David. I owe him that at least—'

She broke off, her breath catching in her throat, and, staring at her pale face, Rollo felt a dull ache of misery beating beneath his anger.

He'd told her there was nothing left to say.

What he'd really meant was that, trapped in the limo with his anger and his memories, he hadn't known how to say it.

Every time he'd tried to start a sentence it had turned into a minefield—his usual effortless fluency deserting him, every word fraught with possible implications. So he'd done what he always did when faced with doubt and discord. He'd walked away.

Stalking down Madison Avenue towards his offices, he'd tried to clear his mind and focus on the afternoon's agenda. Only he'd been too wound up, his body vibrating with leftover adrenalin, his brain frenziedly trying to work out *how* a pitch-perfect lunch had turned into Armageddon.

And *when* suddenly, incredibly he'd stopped caring about work and started caring about his relationship with Daisy.

He took a step forward.

'You don't need to see David,' he said quietly.

'Yes, I do.' She stared at him wildly, her body shuddering, straining for breath. 'I've let him down and he doesn't even know it.'

The ache in her voice seemed to mirror the ache inside his chest.

'You haven't let him down. You saved him.'

'No, I *tried* to save him—to make everything right, to make this work with you—only now you're going to call the police—'

She was babbling, the words tumbling over each other in a torrent so fast that he had to hold up his hand to stop the flow.

'Wait. *Wait.*' He frowned, her breathless panic driving away the last of his anger. 'I'm not going to call the police. I never was.'

Blood was rushing to his head, joining the clamouring voices telling him not to let her leave.

He took a step closer. 'I know what I said. How it must have sounded. But I was angry. I don't like scenes…'

He hesitated, unnerved by this sudden further breach in his defences. He never confided in anyone, and yet this was the second time he'd done so with Daisy in the space of a couple of hours.

'Look, nothing's changed. I didn't come back to end our relationship. I came back to finish our argument. But that's all it is. An argument. It's what couples do, isn't it?'

His heart gave a jolt. *Couple* was a word he'd consciously avoided his whole adult life. And an argument had always been just something to win. Only winning this time would mean losing Daisy, and he wasn't prepared to let that happen.

Had he been thinking straight that thought would

have shocked him. But he was too distracted by Daisy's reaction, or rather the lack of it, to care.

She was staring at him, eyes huge, their brownness lost in the stunned black pupils. Then slowly she shook her head.

'But that's just it. We're not a couple. We're not anything.' She breathed out unsteadily. 'I don't even know who I am half the time, or what's real and what's not.' She met his gaze. 'And it's not just me. Earlier, I was upset—'

He opened his mouth to speak, but she held up her hand to stop him. 'I know it wasn't rational or fair. But I *was*. Only you didn't realise. You thought I was acting.'

A silence fell over the room.

'And that bothers you?'

His question caught her off guard. She stared up at him wearily.

'Yes. Maybe it shouldn't, but it does.' Her mouth twisted. 'I thought the boundaries would be clearer. That I'd feel different when I was being me without you. But it's all merging and—'

She stopped.

Now it's even more complicated, she finished the sentence inside her head.

Thinking back to how he'd touched her, her frantic response, she felt her cheeks start to burn. She'd had other lovers but it had never been like that—so urgent, so feverish. In the space of a few heated moments Rollo had blotted out the past and obliterated every sexual experience she'd had.

But she would rather run down Madison Avenue naked than let him know how strongly he affected her.

Swallowing hard, she reached down, picked up the ring and held it out to him. 'Here. This is yours.'

Rollo stared at her outstretched hand and then slowly took the small gold hoop.

The limpid brown of her eyes heightened the flush of colour on her cheeks. She had never looked more beautiful. But it wasn't her beauty that was making his heart pound.

It was her bravery. He knew how much it would take for him even to admit weakness, let alone reveal his deepest fears. He glanced down at the ring, turning it over gently in the palm of his hand. It was such a small thing. Easy to lose and, once lost, almost impossible to find.

Like trust.

He felt her eyes on his face and glanced away, his thoughts converging and then separating like the colours in a kaleidoscope. He'd made a deal with Daisy—and what kind of deal could ever succeed without trust?

Slowly he reached out and took her hand.

'No, it's yours. I chose it for you.' Something shifted in his face, the skin tightening over his cheekbones. 'And I didn't mean to upset you. That's why I came back. To tell you that.'

Daisy stared at him dazedly. It wasn't an apology. But it was the nearest a man like Rollo Fleming would get to one. And whatever it was, he had come after her to say it.

She watched his mouth curve into an almost smile.

'But if you really don't want it, I suppose I could turn it into a tiepin.'

'I do want it.' Her lashes flickered up and, not giving herself a chance to have second thoughts, she said quickly, 'And I want you.'

There was a fraction of a pause and then slowly he slid the ring onto her finger. And then, breathing out, he drew her close to him so she could feel his heart beating in time to hers.

'And I want you too.'

For a moment they stood together in silence, and

then she felt him shift against her and, looking up, she saw he was frowning.

'What is it?'

'I'm late for a meeting.' His eyes met hers.

'So go,' she said lightly. 'I'll be here when you get back. I'm not going anywhere.'

She felt his arm tighten around her waist, the muscles in his chest growing rigid.

'No, you're not. But *we* are.'

She stared at him, confused. 'We are?'

'Let's get out of here.' He glanced around the apartment, his face creasing. 'Out of Manhattan. Go somewhere we don't have to pretend.'

Her pulse shivered with excitement. 'Where do you have in mind?'

He smiled slowly and her heart contracted sharply with pity for any poor woman who might truly love Rollo. With beauty and charm like his, it was easy to forget his ruthless determination. But, looking up into his smooth, handsome face, she knew he would always be one step ahead of her. And she would be exactly where he wanted her to be.

'I have a small cabin upstate—in the Adirondacks. It's a bit rough and ready, but what do you think? You and me in the wilderness together?'

It sounded like a question, except she knew he didn't expect or need a reply. But as heat uncoiled inside her, she lifted her mouth to his and gave him her answer.

'I should warn you there are bears in the woods. Black bears. They're a lot smaller than grizzlies, and they rarely bother humans, but you should be careful just the same.'

Leaning forward, Rollo picked up his coffee cup. Having arrived at Mohawk Lodge just twenty minutes earlier, they were relaxing in front of a panoramic view of the lake and the Adirondack Mountains beyond. In the distance the forest looked like the setting for a fairy tale but Daisy barely noticed the view.

She was still reeling from the trip in his private helicopter. Or rather, the way Rollo had held her hand during the entire flight, his leg pressing against hers, his mouth temptingly close as he pointed out landmarks and filled her in on the history of the region.

She nodded, then frowned. 'Did you say bears?'

He put his cup down carefully, his eyes narrowing.

'What's up?'

'Nothing.' She met his gaze, then sighed. 'I just didn't realise your whole life was like this.'

'Like what?'

'Like… So amazing.'

He shrugged. 'I don't really think about it.'

'I suppose you get used to it,' she said slowly.

But somehow she couldn't imagine a life in which owning a helicopter and a lakeside cabin would ever be anything other than incredible. It was another reminder of the differences between them.

But right now she needed to concentrate on what they shared, not on what they didn't, and, putting her cup down, she said brightly, 'So how about that guided tour you promised me?'

The cabin was delightful. Set in seventy-five acres of unspoilt meadows and forest, it was built of timber and stone but it shared the same high-spec luxury as the penthouse. And letting Rollo show her around had been the right decision. As they walked outside onto the deck, where a swing bed swayed gently in the warm breeze, her stomach tumbled over with happiness as she felt his hand close around hers.

'So, do you fancy a swim?'

She frowned. 'I don't know. What's the water like?' she said cautiously.

'Probably quite mild.'

Glancing up at his face, she rolled her eyes. 'I might need a second opinion before I whip out my bikini. I'm not entirely sure I trust your judgement.'

Lifting her hand, he tipped it sideways so that the stones in the ring caught the light.

'I thought you liked your ring.'

'I do.' She pinched his fingers playfully. 'I was talking about this place. You said it was a "small cabin."' Glancing inside at the huge stone fireplace and vaulted, beamed ceiling, she shook her head. '"A bit rough and ready," you said. I was expecting bare floors and no electricity.'

Not a soaking tub and a French chef.

Looking up, she fell silent. He was staring at her steadily, eyes dark and unblinking, and then he tugged her towards him and she clutched at his arms as her legs seemed to slide away.

'I can do rough,' he murmured and, lowering his head, he brushed his mouth across hers. Fingers splaying around her waist, he pulled her closer, his breath warm against her throat. 'And I'm certainly ready.'

Her head was spinning… Her body melting like wax near a flame.

Only not with longing but with shame.

Picturing the way he'd pulled away from her, knowing how impossible it would have been for her to do the same, she felt a flicker of doubt and fear.

He felt it too and, lifting his head, his gaze focused steadily on her face.

'What is it?'

She hesitated, her eyes shying away from his. She wanted him so badly. But she couldn't give herself to him. Not now she knew his desire was motivated by power, not passion.

'Daisy? *Daisy?*'

His voice was insistent, inexorable. It was a voice she could not refuse.

'Yesterday when we… When you—'

She frowned. There was a tremor in her voice and she knew that her eyes were bright with tears.

'I know you wanted sex. But I also know that you didn't want *me*.'

It had been a guess—a theory. But as he gazed down at her in silence she felt a rush of misery so intense that she couldn't bear to look at him. Pushing against his chest, she edged away, fixing her gaze on the shimmering mass of water.

'You're wrong.'

She lifted her face to his, her heart leaden in her chest.

'So why did you stop?'

How could you stop? she wanted to ask, remembering the strength and the violence of her longing for him. How could he have been so coolly detached?

But, glancing at his handsome face, she thought he looked anything but detached now. Instead he looked strained and unsure.

He shook his head, the skin tightening across his cheekbones.

'Short answer—I'm an idiot. I wanted to prove to myself you were *optional*. That demonstrating my willpower was more satisfying than you could ever be. But I was wrong. On both counts.' He grimaced. 'The last twenty-four hours have been the most uncomfortable of my entire life. And all I managed to prove is that I can't actually function because I want you so badly.'

She breathed out, her heart pounding with a mix of shock and relief and a stunned, helpless happiness.

But she wasn't going to make it easy for him. He had hurt her. And, yes, she knew it was because he hated losing control. But he had to understand that although that might be a reason for his behaviour it didn't excuse it.

'How do I know that's true? That you want me? You might be pretending.'

His eyes narrowed and then her heart rate seemed to double as he pulled her firmly against him and she felt the hard length of his erection pressing against her.

'Trust me, Daisy. This is real. And it's for you. Just you.'

Reaching out, he touched her face gently and the warmth of his fingertips sent a tremor through her body.

'You're all I think about. All I've been thinking about since I kissed you in my office. It's like I'm living from one moment to the next. But if you won't believe what I say then maybe I'll just have to show you instead.'

And, lowering his mouth, he kissed her. It was a kiss like no other. Hotter, deeper. And his mouth possessed her with a ferocity that wiped out all conscious thought.

As his hands moved lightly over her back and shoulders and neck she shivered beneath their touch, head swimming, body swaying against his as he nudged her backwards. She bumped into the swing, felt wood scraping her bare legs, and then, slipping his hands around her waist, he lifted her up onto the mattress.

His hands were urgent against her skin, pulling off her boots, her T-shirt, and somehow her jeans came off too and she was suddenly naked except for her underwear.

Her breath caught in her throat as he leaned over her, his face tensed with passion and something softer, less guarded. And she knew that he wanted her to see what he was feeling, to know it was real.

In a heartbeat, her doubts were forgotten. His hunger was her hunger. Only it was more than hunger. It was like being consumed by fire—total and complete surrender to the flame of passion that burned between them.

She stared up into his face. 'Kiss me,' she whispered.

His eyes on hers were the dark green of the forest across the water and, leaning forward, he kissed her slowly, his tongue probing between her lips, delicate and deliberate, so that heat stabbed inside her.

'Open your mouth,' he muttered. 'I want to taste you.'

He was barely breathing, his head empty and

hollow of anything except the pulse beating in his groin.

As the late afternoon sun spread over the deck, liquid gold spilled over her skin and he felt his last atom of self-control dissolve.

He dipped his head, dipped and licked inside her mouth, his teeth nipping, tugging her swollen lips. And, moaning softly, she kissed him back, her fingers digging into his scalp, pulling him closer and deeper until he broke away panting, his eyes blunt and unfocused.

For a moment he stared at her in silence, dazed, dry-mouthed, almost drunk on her beauty, then slowly he cupped her breast in his hand, his thumb brushing against the tip of her nipple, and the blood gathered thickly inside him as he watched her face soften.

Daisy shuddered. A thread of heat was stretching out inside her and suddenly she was arching upwards, her thighs trembling. She felt him push aside the flimsy fabric of her bra, felt his mouth closing over her breast and then his fingers were slipping over her body, across her stomach and hips and between her legs, clasping the pulsing ache against the palm of his hand.

Her breath thickened in her throat. Suddenly she

was clawing at his belt, her nails scraping against the denim of his jeans, tugging the zip down, her whole body vibrating with need as her fingers found the smooth hardness of his erection.

At the touch of her hand his body jerked involuntarily and groaning, he lifted his mouth and shifted against her, reaching into his pocket for a condom, fingers tearing clumsily at the wrapper. And then he was smoothing it on, feeling himself grow thicker and harder.

Maddened, she clutched at him frantically, her back curving upwards, seeking more of his mouth and his hands, as he tugged her underwear to one side. The weight of his body was pressing down on her and into her and she rocked against him, her face buried in his shoulder, the pulse inside her beating wildly.

He shifted his hips and she felt a sharp sting of ecstasy and tensing, she shuddered against him. And then his mouth found hers and, groaning her name against her lips, he pushed up, driving into her hard and fast while her body still contracted around his.

Later, bodies still entwined, they watched a rose-coloured sun sink behind the mountains. Breathing out softly, Daisy ran her hand lightly over his stomach.

'This place is so remote. How did you come across it?'

'I did a deal a few years ago with a guy called Tim Buchanan. He and I enjoyed the same kind of activities, so he invited me up here for a weekend.'

She raised an eyebrow. 'Activities! Sounds intriguing!' She gave him a small teasing smile. 'You're not one of those role play fanatics, are you? You know—the kind who re-enact the Civil War. I won't come out of the shower and find you dressed as Abraham Lincoln, will I?'

His eyes gleamed. 'I meant shooting and fishing. But I'm always up for a bit of role play.'

His fingers tiptoed over the curve of her hip and a hot shiver slid over her skin, her body responding both to his touch and the teasing note in his voice. 'Well, let me know and I'll unpack my crinoline,' she said lightly.

Glancing back across the lake, she sighed.

'You're so lucky it was for sale.'

'It wasn't. But I liked it, so I made him an offer and he accepted.'

She nodded, as though she too was in the habit of purchasing lakeside mansions on a whim.

'Your family must love it.'

Even before she heard the edge in his voice she could feel a slight tensing in his shoulders.

'I'm sure they would have done. But both my parents are gone.'

How had she not known that? He knew all about her family. But somehow his past had never come up for discussion. Or maybe he had chosen to keep it to himself.

'Oh, I'm sorry.'

And she was. The thought of losing one of her parents filled her with dread—to lose both seemed intolerable.

'But they must have been so proud of you and everything you've achieved.'

This time his hesitation was unmistakable. For a minute she thought he wasn't going to answer. Finally, though, he gave her a perfunctory smile.

'Isn't every parent?'

He didn't move, but she could almost feel him retreating from her. Nodding mechanically, she decided it was time to change the subject.

'Do you think we could sleep out here tonight?'

She felt him relax.

'I guess so.' His gaze locked on to hers. 'Won't

you be scared though? Like I said, there are wild animals out here.'

'They don't scare me,' she said huskily. 'I know how to tame them.' And, wriggling closer, she climbed on top of him, catching his wrists with her hands.

'Are you sure?'

His voice was hoarse, his eyes dark and fierce, and she could feel the pulse beating beneath his skin.

'Yes,' she murmured. 'Only I might need a bit more practice.'

'Good idea. Practice makes—'

But he broke off on a gasp as, lowering her mouth, she ran her tongue lightly over the smooth muscles of his chest, then lower, down the line of soft golden hair on his stomach, and then lower still...

Afterwards, she lay in his arms, watching him sleep. She felt drowsy but she didn't want to close her eyes. Or for the moment to end.

All her life she'd been searching for passion. Looking for that intensity of feeling, that intimacy of knowing somebody inside out.

Only she'd never imagined finding it with Rollo.

At best, she'd assumed that being with him would offer a respite from the heartbreak of another failed romance. What she hadn't expected was this incredible sexual chemistry—a physical attraction that filled her with wonder and yearning.

It might not be love.

It might not be permanent.

But right now she was living in the moment.

And she was going to make the most of it.

As the warmth of his body seeped into her she curled her arm more tightly over his chest and, closing her eyes, fell instantly asleep.

CHAPTER EIGHT

IGNORING THE BURNING ache in his lungs, Rollo sprinted up the hill. Only another couple of metres to go and—

A small but intrusive alarm broke through the pounding of his heart and, slowing to a jog, he headed towards the wooden jetty that stretched out into the lake. His arms were shaking, the T-shirt he was wearing was damp with sweat, but the heat and chaos of his body felt inconsequential beside the turmoil inside his head.

He had woken early, eyes straining against the first sliver of light slicing through the blinds. There was nothing unusual about that. The business world was always awake somewhere in the world, and he routinely made property deals at all hours of the day and night. Normally, he found it easy to get up early.

But this time he'd been oddly reluctant to move. He'd felt warm and comfortable and it had been easy to lie there, drowsily listening to the sound of the waves lapping against the deck.

Only beneath his lethargy and the comforting rhythm of the water there had been a nagging sense of something being different.

It had taken him a moment to realise that the difference was Daisy.

Or, more particularly, the fact that at some point during the night her soft body had curled against his. And he hadn't pushed her away.

For a moment his mind had stalled. He had felt wrong-footed by the sudden, new and unsettling state of affairs. As a red-blooded male, wanting sex was hot-wired into his DNA. But waking up beside a woman was something he'd taken extreme care to avoid throughout his adult life.

Yet there she'd been, legs tangled between his, her hand curling over his waist—

From somewhere in the forest the sharp cry of a bird jolted his mind back into real time. Leaning forward against the railing, he stared dazedly across the water, trying to make sense of his behaviour.

It took several minutes for him to concede that it might have something to do with Daisy. Or rather sex with Daisy.

His skin tightened and he felt an almost unbearable tug of sexual anticipation, just as he had during the night, when it had been impossible not to reach over and pull her into his arms.

It had been wild, heated, mind-blowing, and she had made him want more, give more, feel more than any woman he had known before. Her feverish demands had matched his, her hands, lips, body had been like quicksilver. Even now, with the cool breeze blowing across the water, he could feel the white-hot imprint of her touch on his skin—

But nothing had really changed, he reassured himself. Daisy might look like a sleeping princess, with her long, blonde hair spread out over the pillows, but there would be no fairy-tale ending to their relationship.

Yes, he would marry her. But only because he needed a wife to persuade Dunmore to sell to him. Although after last night, she felt more like a compulsion than a necessity.

Remembering her smooth, naked body, and his own speechless, almost savage exultation at the way she had melted into him, he felt himself grow instantly and painfully hard.

Breathing out slowly, he frowned. There it was

again: that same nagging uneasiness that had woken him. The sense that Daisy was different.

That he was different when he was with her.

But why? It wasn't as though he'd lived a life of celibacy. He'd had many women. All beautiful and sexually eager, and at the time he had wanted them—some of them badly. But never like this. Never with this relentless, excruciating hunger. And never once that hunger had been sated. Walking away had always been easy. Only not this time. Not with Daisy.

His mouth twisted. He'd had to force himself to get up this morning. And he'd only done it to prove to himself that she was an indulgence he could resist.

But instead her absence was like an actual physical pain. Every nerve, every sense focusing in on it, like a toothache.

He frowned. Sex with Daisy was supposed to cure his sexual frustration, not exacerbate it. Only it appeared that instead of having his appetite sated he had grown instantly and intensely addicted to her.

Probably it was because he'd never gone without sex for so long, or had to deal with so much intimacy. And so what if it was taking longer than usual to work her out of his system? He had a whole year to wear her out in his bed.

In the meantime, however, he needed to be careful. Disciplined. Pragmatic. It would be easy to lose himself in his desire for Daisy, but he must not lose sight of the real reason she was in his bed. Or the fact that once Dunmore signed over that building to him she would be gone from his life for ever.

And turning away from the lake, he began a leisurely jog back along the jetty towards the lodge.

'What's this?'

Gazing up at Rollo, Daisy stifled a yawn. 'What's what?' she asked sleepily.

He never seemed to tire of touching her, and now he was caressing her leg, his hand moving slowly down from her hip.

After he'd returned from his run he'd showered and woken her impatiently and they had made love for most of the morning. Now they were lying in bed together, their skin hot and damp, their bodies exhausted. Or rather *she* was exhausted. Rollo seemed energised by the morning's activities.

'What's what?' she said again.

'This.'

She felt his fingers stop and slowly trace a figure of eight on the skin above her knee, and instantly she forgot her question, forgot his answer, forgot who and where she was. Her whole body was trembling, nipples tightening, a soft, liquid heat spreading inside her so that she could hardly breathe, could barely control the longing spilling over her skin.

She stared at him dazedly, hardly daring to believe he was there beside her, all sleek, warm muscle and smooth, golden limbs. He was just so gorgeous, and he made her feel gorgeous too.

Not just gorgeous, but somehow freer and truer to herself.

With other boyfriends—with everyone, really, except David sometimes—she felt as though she was always pretending to be someone else. Someone she didn't want to be—happy-go-lucky, ditsy Daisy, who never quite pulled it off, whether 'it' was a relationship or her career.

But with Rollo, it was different.

She felt different.

Unsurprisingly, she thought grimly. Even aside from his being one of the richest men in the country, it wasn't exactly a run-of-the-mill relationship. Her other boyfriends might have been lazy and thoughtless and immature, but none had black-mailed her into playing their wife.

But it wasn't just the framework of their relationship that was making her feel so blindsided. It was Rollo himself—or rather the way he demanded a truthfulness, an honesty, that other men did not. Not just with facts but with herself. With him there was nowhere to hide. He wanted all of her. The good, the bad and the pretend-it-never-happened. No one had ever got under her skin and turned her inside out like that.

It made her feel helpless, off balance, and yet in his arms she felt warm and secure, all her old fears and doubts about herself kept at bay by the steady beat of his heart.

She felt her own heartbeat stumble as a flush of heat crept over her cheeks.

That was the trouble with sex.

She'd been there before, and each time it had been the same old story. Sex felt so *intimate*. And it was—physically. Only really it was nothing but bodies wrapping round one another.

She frowned. It sounded if not bleak, then mechanical, and not at all like the way she had felt with Rollo. But then sex with him had been beyond anything she'd ever imagined. She'd never responded to any man like that—so fiercely, so freely. It was exhilarating—and terrifying. At times she couldn't even recognise herself. Who was this woman who initiated and demanded so much? But it had felt good to be that woman. To be herself—the Daisy she had wanted to be for so many years.

Her thoughts slowed.

Being with Rollo felt right in other ways too. Maybe it was because they shared a secret. But it felt as though they knew other well. Almost as though they had been reunited after a long separation. Which was not only untrue, she admitted ruefully, but also made no sense whatsoever.

She felt his gaze on her face and, pushing aside her thoughts, she glanced to where his fingers were still doodling over her skin.

'Oh, that.' It was a small cut just above her knee. She felt a flush of heat rise over her face. 'That's where I banged into that board thing in your office.'

Beside her, Rollo tilted his head back, her words acting like an emergency brake on his runaway desire. His office! His hand trembled slightly against the scar on her leg.

How could he have forgotten how they met? Or

the real reason she was here in his bed. He felt a flicker of irritation that he'd let his libido get in the way of business.

'That reminds me—James Dunmore rang. He's invited us to lunch. Apparently he very much wants to meet you.'

Daisy stared at him in silence. There was an expression on his face she didn't quite recognise, and momentarily she thought it might be regret.

But his next statement instantly dispelled that idea.

'Holiday's over,' he said casually. 'Time to go back to work.'

His words echoed inside her head.

It hadn't felt like a holiday. It had felt like a honeymoon. Either way, though, it was over.

Forcing herself to smile, she met his gaze.

'That's great,' she said quickly. 'I'll go and get dressed. We don't want to keep him waiting.'

As the helicopter rose upwards, Daisy glanced furtively at the time on her phone. Her heart was beating nervously. Now that she was actually about to meet him, she would have liked more time to get to know the man for whom this charade was happening.

Damping down her panic, she cleared her throat. 'Is there anything I should know about Mr Dunmore? I mean, I know the basics, but—'

Turning, Rollo stared at her, his cool expression a clear indication that the relaxed lover of the past few days had been replaced by the dispassionate property tycoon.

'The basics will do just fine.'

He glanced back out the window.

Beneath them, the soft green of the forest was growing sparser. Roads were starting to crisscross the landscape. Soon he would be shaking hands with Dunmore, Daisy by his side. It was the moment he'd been working towards all his life—the moment when his goal switched from impossible dream to possible reality.

So why, then, did he want nothing more than to turn back time? To go back to the lodge and it be just be the two of them.

It was nerves, he told himself quickly, his gaze tugging towards where Daisy sat, wearing a navy pencil skirt, a gold chain belt accentuating the waistline of her fitted grey blouse. Nerves and a raging, unassailable lust for the tempting body that lay beneath that demure outfit.

Pushing aside his desire, he cleared his throat.

'Dunmore's been married to the same woman since he was nineteen. He's a romantic.'

He smiled, but Daisy couldn't bring herself to smile back. The dismissive tone in his voice, his barely masked incredulity that a man could truly love a woman, let alone choose to stay with her, for life tasted bitter in her mouth.

But it wasn't her problem, she reminded herself quickly. Maybe if theirs was a real relationship, his emotional disconnect would matter. But thankfully she would never have to endure the pain of loving Rollo. What she felt for him was just simple and shallow: lust.

Perhaps he registered the effect of his words, for when he spoke again she saw that the mockery in his eyes had faded.

'You'll be fine. He's a nice man who just wants to hear about you—about us. All you have to do is pretend you're madly in love with me.'

He shifted closer, his hand tightening on hers, and suddenly her mouth was dry, her heart hammering, her entire body so aware of him and only him that for a moment the noise of the helicopter faded away and it was as though they were flying through the air alone together.

'Is that all?' Their eyes met and she managed to

smile. 'In that case, no problem. You can be Romeo and I'll just channel my inner Juliet.'

He laughed softly and she felt a rush of pleasure. Not just because she had made him laugh, but at the way his body was sprawled against hers. There was a take-it-for-granted intimacy to it that would have been impossible only a few days before.

'Both of us dying over lunch seems a little extreme.'

'That's where you're wrong,' she said lightly, glancing out of the window at the skyscrapers below. 'It can't be true love unless someone dies or ends up alone and heartbroken.'

Turning back, she expected him still to be smiling. But instead his eyes were fixed on her face, his expression serious and oddly intense.

'I thought you believed in happy-ever-after,' he said quietly.

The stillness in the cabin seemed to press against her so that suddenly she was painfully aware of her own breathing.

'I did. I do—'

A pulse of tension was beating beneath her skin. Staring at him in confusion, she rewound their conversation, searching for an explanation for this abrupt change of mood.

Then from somewhere behind her head the intercom crackled and the voice of the pilot split the silence.

'Just to let you know we'll be landing in about five minutes, sir. There's a slight breeze, but other than that it looks like it's going to be a beautiful day.'

Moments later the helicopter touched down on the roof of one of Manhattan's many skyscrapers, and then they were walking across the concrete, her heels tapping like castanets.

'This way, Mr Fleming… Ms Maddox.'

A bodyguard in a dark suit stepped forward, gesturing towards the lift. Watching the numbers change as the lift descended, Daisy felt her stomach tighten. It was almost the moment of truth. The moment she found out if all that preparation had paid off and the audience believed her performance.

She breathed out silently.

Everything should be all right. She knew his back story the way she knew her own life, and her body still pulsed with the aftershock of his lovemaking.

And yet something was wrong.

Beside her, Rollo was silent, his face expressionless. But something in the way he was holding his body made her instantly forget her own nerves.

'Rollo—'

He didn't answer and she held her breath, feeling almost as she had when she'd broken into his office. Only this time it was clear she was intruding on something deeper. She felt a sudden slippery panic slither over her skin. If she felt like an intruder, how were they ever going to convince Dunmore that their relationship was real?

'Rollo. It's going to be okay.'

'I know.'

The distance in his voice caught her off guard. But before she could respond, the lift doors opened and she felt his hand on her arm. And then he was guiding her forward, past another bodyguard into a large, open-plan living space where two men stood talking casually by the window.

She stopped abruptly. 'Rollo—'

Behind them she felt the bodyguard discreetly retreat as Rollo turned to face her.

A muscle flickered in his jaw. 'Are you trying to make us late?'

It was an accusation dressed up as a question. But with a sting of shock, she realised it was more than that. It was a justification—a reason to be angry. But why did Rollo need to be *angry*?

And then, looking into his eyes, she felt a sudden painful tightening in her chest as she realised that it wasn't anger he was feeling. It was fear. He was afraid of blowing the deal.

Instinctively she stepped forward and, taking his hand, squeezed it between her fingers.

'I know how much this matters to you. It matters to me too, and together we can make it work. So please don't push me away.'

As the silence stretched between them she thought he might do just that. But he didn't. Instead, after a brief hesitation, his fingers tightened around hers.

'I'm sorry,' he said quietly.

She breathed out sharply.

'Good.' Her eyes flared. 'You should be. From now on it's you and me against the world, right?'

As he nodded, she leaned forward and kissed him fiercely. When finally she drew back, some of the tension had left his face.

'Was that for luck?' he said softly.

She shook her head. 'We don't need luck. I just wanted to kiss you. And now I want you to take me to lunch.'

* * *

Halfway through her starter of *burrata pugliese* and wild strawberries, Daisy decided that James Dunmore was one of the nicest men she had ever met. Tall, with greying red hair, he was reassuringly unpretentious and far less intimidating than she'd expected given his wealth and status.

As they'd walked across the living room, he had greeted them warmly, thanked them both for joining him, and then immediately apologised for his wife's absence.

'Emily was so looking forward to seeing you again, Rollo, and, of course, to meeting you, Daisy. Unfortunately her sister was taken ill at the weekend, so she flew up to Vermont to be with her.'

He'd turned to the red-haired man standing next to him.

'But on the plus side, I've managed to coerce my nephew, Jack, into joining us. He heads up my East Coast legal department.'

Jack stepped forward. 'Hey, Rollo, good to meet you.'

'And this is Daisy.'

Dunmore's blue eyes had gleamed. 'I must admit to having an ulterior motive for inviting Jack to join us today. When I heard that Rollo had got engaged I wanted a witness to the transformation. And, of course, to meet the woman who finally tamed him.'

Rollo had smiled coolly. 'I think my reputation may have been somewhat exaggerated by the media.'

'Well, I like mine,' Daisy had said softly. 'The woman who tamed Rollo Fleming! That would look great on a T-shirt, don't you think?'

Dunmore had laughed. 'It certainly would. Now, why don't we eat? I hope you're hungry, Daisy. I'm supposed to be watching my weight, but my chef, Jordi, makes it extremely difficult.'

The food was delicious. But after spending so much time around reserved Manhattan socialites, it was James Dunmore's company that Daisy enjoyed most. He was warm and relaxed and, although he was the CEO of a property empire, it was clear he saw himself as a husband and father first.

'So, Jack is your brother's son?' Leaning back to let the waiter clear her plate, Daisy glanced critically from Dunmore to his nephew. 'He looks just like you. Except—'

'He's got all his own teeth.'

She laughed. 'I was going to say that he's got a different jawline.'

Dunmore frowned. 'That's true. Not many people notice that. They just see the hair—or what's left of it. You're very perceptive, Daisy.'

Smiling, she shrugged. 'I'm an actress. Sometimes the right jawline gets you the part.'

The older man ran a hand through his hair. 'Being red-headed runs in the family. Jack's father and I used to get mistaken for one another a lot when we were younger.'

Daisy looked up curiously. 'But you're not twins?'

He shook his head. 'Oddly enough, we actually have different mothers. But we both take after our dad.'

Leaning forward, Rollo laid his hand over hers. 'Daisy has a twin. Her brother, David.'

'A twin brother!' Dunmore beamed. 'You must have a very intuitive understanding of men.' He glanced pointedly across the table at Rollo. 'That must come in handy.'

Daisy smiled. 'I wish it did. But David is nothing like Rollo.'

Or was he?

Not so long ago likening her uptight, sensitive

brother to Rollo Fleming would have seemed utterly far-fetched. Now, though, it didn't seem nearly as implausible. Rollo might appear autocratic and ruthless, but she had seen another side to him. Nervous, less guarded and kind too—particularly to her brother.

Pushing aside that disconcerting train of thought, she lifted up her glass. 'He's nothing like me either.'

'But you're close?'

'Very.' She nodded. 'We were inseparable when we were little. We still are. But we're very different. Not just in looks but personality, interests. I don't know what I'd do without him. He's like my conscience—always there inside my head.'

'Sorry to butt in.'

It was Jack. He smiled at Daisy and then turned towards his uncle.

'That was a message from Tom Krantz.'

Dunmore frowned. 'Sorry, Daisy, would you excuse me? I wouldn't normally let business interrupt, but—'

'You don't need to explain.'

Taking a sip of water, she smiled. But inside, her heart beat out a percussive rhythm of guilt.

David.

Her brother.

Her twin, who was always inside her head.

Once upon a time that might have been true. But she'd barely given David a thought over the last few days. Instead all fraternal concern had been blotted out by lust and self-absorption.

Lowering her glass she was suddenly conscious of the silence across the table.

Looking up, she met Rollo's gaze.

'I know you miss David. And I know you're worried about him,' he said softly, letting his fingers close around hers.

He envied the closeness she shared with her brother. The absolute trust and dependence. It was pure and powerful and unbreakable.

His chest grew tight. Or it was supposed to be anyway. He forced a smile.

'But he's going to be okay. I'll make sure of that.'

Daisy nodded. His hand felt warm. But it was the warmth and the certainty in his voice that eased the pain in her heart as Dunmore turned back towards her.

After coffee, they sat and chatted easily, until finally Rollo glanced at his watch.

'We really ought to be getting back.'

'Of course.' Standing up, Dunmore patted Rollo

on the shoulder. 'But on one condition. I insist that you both come up to Swan Creek for the weekend. We'll have lunch, and then maybe, Rollo, we can have another look at that proposal of yours.'

CHAPTER NINE

BACK AT THE PENTHOUSE, they tumbled into bed. It was fast and urgent, both of them gripped by the same hot desperation, furiously goading each other with their hands and mouths and bodies, until finally they shuddered to an explosive climax together.

Afterwards, Rollo gathered her against his damp body and, breathing out softly, drifted instantly into sleep.

Beside him though, Daisy lay wide awake. Beneath the beating of her heart Dunmore's offer was playing on a loop inside her head.

'*Maybe, Rollo, we can have another look at that proposal of yours.*'

Rollo had played it cool. He had shown no hint of triumph. But she knew that the older man's words were exactly what he had been hoping to hear. What she too should have been pleased to hear. After all, the quicker Dunmore agreed to sell to Rollo, the sooner she would be free of him.

Only she didn't feel pleased. In fact, being one step closer to Rollo achieving his goal, and thus to her freedom, was making her nerves twitch so that being still was suddenly an impossibility.

What she needed was an anaesthetic—a way to numb her brain. A few rigorous laps of the roof-top pool should do the trick.

Gently lifting Rollo's arm, she slid off the bed and padded towards the dressing room.

Ten minutes later, she was sliding through the clear blue water, her mind so focused on the rhythm of her stroke that soon her anxieties faded away. Finally she could swim no more and, heart pounding, she pulled herself out onto the deck.

As she wiped the water from her eyes her heart did a backflip. Rollo was sitting on one of the loungers, wearing jeans, his feet and chest bare, a towel dangling from his hand.

She smiled. 'I thought you were asleep.'

'I was. But I woke up and you were gone.'

There was a tension in his voice she might have missed had she not grown so attuned to the subtleties of his manner.

'I was a bit wound up,' she said lightly. 'So I went for a swim.'

His eyes rested on her face. 'What's up? Are you still worrying about David?'

She was about to nod automatically, but with shock she realised that she wasn't. She had spoken to her parents and her brother on the way back to the apartment, and they'd been surprised—particularly David—by the news of her engagement. But as she'd expected their happiness had outweighed any misgivings. She felt calmer about everything except—

She shook her head. 'It's not David. It's James. Mr Dunmore.'

His gaze searched her face with a hint of impatience.

'What about him?'

She shrugged. 'I don't know. I suppose he wasn't real before. Now he is. And I liked him,' she said simply.

'And that's a problem?' His fingers tapped irritably against the arm of the chair.

She caught her breath, his impatience stirring irritation of her own. 'Yes. I don't like lying to someone I like and respect.'

His eyes narrowed. 'I'm sure you'll still "like and respect" him when he agrees to sell to me.'

She stared at him, her heart banging against her

ribs. He was missing the point. Or choosing to miss it.

'It just makes me feel shabby. He's a nice man. He doesn't deserve—'

'Deserve what?' His face was set, the tension in his body now a tangible presence. 'The large sum of money I'm going to pay him? Dunmore's a businessman. If he sells to me, it will be a business decision, not a favour or a charitable bequest.'

She shivered. His whole manner had changed, his face hardening to a mask so that it was all she could do to meet his gaze.

'That's not what you said before,' she said hoarsely. 'You said he'd only sell to someone with the right values. That's why we have to marry, isn't it? So he'll believe you've found love and happiness with the right woman?'

He flinched at her words—or maybe it was the sunlight catching her eye, for when she looked at him again he seemed as poised and cold as before.

'I'm not responsible for what Dunmore believes or feels.'

'What about what you feel?' The blood was humming in her head, a nub of dread chafing beneath her heart. 'I thought you liked him.'

A muscle flickered in his cheek.

'It would make no difference to my decision if I didn't. This is business, and feelings have nothing to do with business.' He stood up abruptly. 'But, more important, neither do you. In case you've forgotten, you're just here to clear a debt.'

Her breath seemed to fray in her chest. *Just here to clear a debt.* It sounded like an epitaph. And in a way it was—an epitaph for her naivety.

Had she really thought having sex with Rollo would change their relationship? She'd been wrong.

They were back to being strangers.

She wanted to rail against her stupid, gullible self for the way she had lain in his arms, opened her body to his, felt—

Her hands started to shake and, balling them into fists, she directed her fury at Rollo instead.

'No, that's *your* reason, Rollo, not mine. I'm here because I love my brother. But do you know something? I'd stay now even if you *weren't* blackmailing me, because I know how much this deal means to you. Perhaps if you cared about anything other than your business and that building, you might understand that. Oh, and you might not have to blackmail a stranger into playing your wife. You might actually be the man you're pretending to be!'

His face was blank, but she could tell he was fighting for control...at the edge of losing his temper.

'You know nothing about me. Or what I care about.'

There was a clear note of warning in his voice and she was glad, for it meant that she had struck a nerve.

'Why? Because I'm just a woman clearing a debt?'

But even as she spoke she knew that it wasn't about her. This was about *him*. About his anger and his arrogance and the mask that came down every time he thought she was getting too close.

'You're wrong, Rollo. I do know what you care about. You care about honesty. Only you're not being honest now about why you're upset with me.'

There was a long, quivering silence. Finally, he breathed out unsteadily. 'Did you mean it? What you said about staying with me?'

She blinked. She hadn't planned on saying those words; they'd sprung from somewhere deep inside. She felt suddenly vulnerable, hearing them repeated back to her. But even if it meant looking foolish and weak, she wasn't going to lie to him.

She nodded. 'But I don't suppose that matters to you any more than I do.'

'You *do* matter…'

'I know.' She spoke coldly, her eyes blazing. 'Without me you won't get your building—'

'No, not because of that…' He hesitated, a tremor moving across his face. 'What I said yesterday—it was true. You're all I think about and—' The skin across his cheekbones was stretched taut; his shoulders rising and falling. 'You're right. I am upset.'

'Because I said I didn't like lying to Dunmore?'

'Yes—no.' His mouth twisted, his fingers curling around the towel. 'It just seemed like you were worried about him and David and *their* feelings and not about me.'

'That's not true.' She breathed out shakily. 'I do care about you. But you don't want me to.'

His hands stilled and for a moment he stared at her in silence. Then he said flatly, 'You're a good person.'

She stared at him uncertainly. 'Not really. It's easy to do the right thing for love.'

'Love?' He frowned, his gaze suddenly intent.

She felt her face grow warmer. 'I meant for David. I love my brother.' She bit her lip. 'I'd do anything for him. For any of my family. That's what matters to me.'

Not that Rollo would ever understand that, she thought wearily. Other than a few offhand remarks, he'd barely discussed his childhood, and his careless exploitation of her relationship with David suggested that family meant nothing to him.

But, glancing over at his face, she felt her heart start to pound. She had expected derision or incomprehension, coldness or anger. But instead he looked stricken.

And suddenly she understood.

'It matters to you too.'

His head jerked up, his eyes widening like an animal's, poised for fight or flight, and instinctively she lowered her voice.

'That's why you want that building, isn't it?'

Her breath caught in her throat as his gaze fixed past her, at some unseen point in the distance. But she knew where he was looking. She'd seen the picture on his desk.

He nodded slowly but didn't reply, and for a moment they stood in silence like actors in the wings, waiting for their cue.

Then finally, he nodded again. 'I used to live there. A long time ago.'

It sounded like the beginning of a fairy tale. But she knew from the strain in his voice that his story would have no happy ending.

'With your parents?' she prompted gently.

He nodded. 'My father wasn't a practical man, but he had ideas. And passion. That's how he met my mother. He was working at a country club as a groundsman and he saw her with her parents. And just like that he knew she was the one. So he cut all the roses he could find and when he gave them to her he asked her to marry him.'

He gave Daisy a small, tight smile.

'He lost his job. But he didn't care because she said yes.'

She nodded, wondering how a smile could be so sad. 'That's so romantic. They must have been very happy.'

His smile tightened. 'He was.' He paused, his eyes bleak. 'My mother not so much. After they got married, they moved to the city. It was hard. My father didn't earn much, and his "ideas" used up all her trust fund. She hated not having money—hated living from day to day. But then when I was about ten, and my sister Rosamund was four, he got a really good job.'

Daisy stared at him in shock. *Sister!* She had

thought he was an only child. But now that he was finally talking so openly she dared not interrupt.

'It was good money, and he rented an apartment for us. It wasn't huge, or fancy. But for the first time my mother was happy. We all were. There was even a playground, with swings and slides, and I used to take Rosamund there all the time. My mom would cook and we'd have dinner as a family and then we'd play cards. It was perfect.'

Her heart contracted at the wonder in his voice. 'What happened?'

He shrugged. 'I don't know. She'd be okay for maybe a month or two, and then she'd start coming home late. Missing meals. Then she'd pack her bags. Threaten to leave.'

Remembering his face when he'd found her with her suitcase, Daisy felt a pang of misery. No wonder he'd reacted so furiously. It must have reminded him of other times—other suitcases.

'And did she?' she said in a small voice.

'No. My father would buy her some gift, or take her out to dinner, and she'd be happy again. He spent so much money trying to make her happy. And then one day they came to the apartment.'

'Who came?' She held her breath, waiting for the answer, even though she knew what it would be.

'The bailiffs.' His face was harder than stone. 'It turned out my father had lost his job months earlier, only he hadn't wanted to tell her. We had to move out. There and then. In front of all the neighbours.'

She swallowed. Her eyes were burning, but not with anger. 'I'm so sorry, Rollo.'

His shoulders were rigid. 'The first time was the worst. Like everything else, it got easier with practice.'

His matter-of-fact tone as much as the implication of his words made her stomach clench painfully, and she had to grit her teeth to stop the tears in her eyes from falling.

'My mother couldn't bear it. She left the week before my thirteenth birthday.'

This time the effort in his smile was too painful to witness and she glanced away, feeling slightly sick.

'There was a note. She blamed my father for being fired, wasting their money, losing the apartment. For ruining her life. I'd heard it all before. But seeing it written down was a lot worse.'

He frowned.

'My dad took it very badly. He felt completely responsible, and he became obsessed with getting the apartment back. He thought if he did, that she'd come home. So he worked and worked. And then one day he collapsed. He was in hospital for a couple of weeks. And then he died.'

His mouth twisted, and without thinking she stepped forward and gripped his hands with hers.

He glanced down at her with a sort of angry bewilderment. 'He made me promise I'd get the apartment back. You see, he still loved her.'

'And you will,' she said firmly. '*We* will.'

His eyes searched her face. 'After everything I've done and said, you still mean that?'

She nodded. 'I do.'

I do.

Her words danced inside her head and she stared past him dazedly. Behind the skyscrapers the sun was shining like a golden orb. But it was dull and shadowy in comparison to the sudden blazing re-alisation that burst into her head like a comet.

She loved him.

Her chest felt hot and tight. Surely she must be mistaken. But no matter how many ways she tried to deny or dispute it she knew she was right. She loved him. Why else would she care so much about his happiness? His dreams. His future.

Only she couldn't think about that now—much less share it with Rollo.

Stepping forward, she slid her arms around him, and after a moment he pulled her close, gripping her tightly. She felt his lips brush against her hair.

'I'm sorry. For what I said and what I didn't say.'

Tipping her head back, she met his gaze. 'It doesn't matter. So what happened afterwards? To your mother?'

She saw the reluctance in his eyes, felt the sudden rigidity in his arms, but after a moment, his muscles loosened.

'I haven't seen or spoken to her for seventeen years. She writes to me, but I don't read the letters. There's no point. Nothing she can say would change what she did.'

Daisy nodded. His words were an echo of what he'd said to her in the limo. He'd been lying then and she knew he was lying now. Only it didn't seem like the right time to point that out.

'But wouldn't your father have wanted her to know about the apartment?' she said carefully. 'For her to know how much he loved her?'

'She knew,' he said tersely. 'My mother left because she was having an affair. She didn't care about my father. She didn't care about me. And she didn't care about the apartment. When she walked out she took what she wanted and left everything else behind. Including me.'

Something shifted in his expression and just for a second she could see the hurt defiance of the boy who'd been abandoned. Helplessly she squeezed his arm. As an actress, she knew how powerful words could be. But what words were there that could undo this kind of damage?

'Maybe she was going to come back later, when she was settled somewhere,' she said haltingly. 'Nobody would want to take a child away from its home.'

'That might depend on the child.' His face was contorted; he sounded drained, defeated.

'She took my sister, so maybe she only really wanted a daughter.'

Daisy breathed in sharply. Suddenly it all made sense.

Thinking back to their first meeting in his office, she felt her stomach clench. He'd been angry— rightfully so, considering he'd just caught her breaking into his office—and she'd assumed his fury would dissipate. But she'd been wrong. Instead it had stayed constant, dark and churning beneath the surface, swift to rise up. And accompanied by a resistance—a refusal to let slip the mask he wore…that hard, smooth golden mask of absolute control.

And now she understood why.

He didn't trust anyone. He didn't believe in love or believe he was worthy of loving. That was why he was scared to commit and care—and why he'd arranged to marry a stranger.

Pain skewered her heart. She stared at him in silence, knowing, feeling, *loving* him. All of him. Especially his angry teenage self. She loved that Rollo as much as, if not more than, the gilded billionaire.

Desperately she searched for something to say—some words that would take the pain from his eyes and the aching misery from his voice. Words that would explain his mother's actions and make him feel better about himself.

But sometimes actions spoke louder than words. And, wrapping her arms around his neck, she kissed him gently.

CHAPTER TEN

SHIFTING BACK IN his seat, Rollo gazed down at his desk, his green eyes narrowing as they focused on the dossier in front of him. Pictured on the smooth, laminated cover was the building of his dreams. It had always been out of his reach, either through lack of finance or lately because of James Dunmore's persistent and frustrating refusal to sell. But, undeterred by the obstacles in his path, he had pursued it relentlessly. And now, the final hurdle was in sight.

Leaning forward, he ran his hand over his company's logo and breathed out softly. Tomorrow he would meet with Dunmore at his Hamptons home to discuss the sale. It was nothing short of a miracle.

And it was all down to Daisy.

Without her he would still be struggling with his image as a serial philanderer. But now his legendary lack of commitment had been rebooted— rebranded as merely the symptom of a man desperately seeking that one special woman with whom to share his life.

As far as everyone was concerned—particularly Dunmore—that woman was Daisy.

Only he knew better.

He knew it was a sham.

Or that was what it was supposed to be.

Lately though, the distinction between reality and pretence felt increasingly hazy and obscure.

He frowned. At first he'd assumed it was a consequence of cohabitation. Now though, his assumption that he could enforce any kind of boundary seemed naive, laughable. Not only had Daisy sneaked past every barrier he'd built between himself and the world, but the devastating sexual attraction they shared had effectively eroded the line between their private and public relationship.

A muscle twitched in his jaw. And now he was losing control of more than just his body. He'd never discussed his private life with anyone before, much less his past. Yet yesterday, with Daisy, he'd turned into some kind of talk-show guest. He'd told her everything—every humiliating little detail.

And she'd listened to each and every word as though it mattered. As though he mattered. And the fact that she'd done that blew his mind almost as much as her admission that he no longer needed to blackmail her into staying. Given how he'd treated her, it was more than he deserved.

He shifted uncomfortably in his seat. He'd been so ruthless—callously exploiting her love for David to get his own way. What kind of man would do that? And how would he feel if someone treated Rosamund with such contempt and disregard?

His chest grew tight.

He'd buried the pain of the past for so many years, but now all of a sudden he couldn't stop thinking about his mother and sister. Picturing Rosamund, her eyes widening with delight as he pushed her on the swing, he gritted his teeth. His anger had made it easy to concentrate on the bad but it was much harder to brush aside happy memories.

However thinking about the past was pointless. There was nothing he could do to change it. The only change that mattered right now was the fact that finally Dunmore was willing to talk terms.

Pushing back his chair, he picked up the dossier and walked purposefully across his office. Every step was bringing him closer to keeping his promise. He should be feeling excited…elated.

And yet all he could think about was what would happen afterwards.

When the contracts were signed.

And when Daisy was extraneous to his life.

Stepping out of the limousine onto the smooth paved driveway in front of Swan Creek, Daisy stopped dead. Rollo's apartment had been a shocking and awe-inspiring revelation of how the other half lived. The Dunmores' Hamptons home took that shock and awe and magnified it tenfold. It was so immense, so impressive, so imposing, that for a moment she wondered if she was actually dreaming.

But then Rollo's hand slid over hers and she knew she was awake.

'I know it doesn't look like it,' he said softly, glancing up to where James Dunmore and his wife, Emily, stood smiling on the steps. 'But to them it's home. Like the penthouse is our home.'

The warmth of his hand matched the warmth in his voice—and the warmth in her heart when he'd said 'our home.'

Since Rollo had confided in her about his past she had found it almost impossible to stop thinking about his mother's behaviour and its devastating impact on her son.

She had thought he wanted the building for profit, or simply to satisfy some baffling masculine need to conquer a business rival. Instead it was all about keeping a promise to his father.

Her throat swelled. Finally she was beginning to understand what had made him the way he was, and everything looked different now. His reticence was no longer a flaw but a teenage boy's perfectly understandable response to being abandoned by his mother. And beneath his ruthless exterior there was a man who was capable of loyalty and love. A man she wanted to get to know so much better.

But she still hadn't told him that her feelings had changed.

So many times over the last few days she'd been on the verge of saying something—words had jostled inside her head, eloquent and clumsy, euphoric and tentative, all jumbling together so that it had been an effort to speak normally at all.

And an impossibility to declare her love.

But maybe that was for the best.

She knew how hard it had been for Rollo to reveal his past. Right now, faced with the chance to make a deal with Dunmore and make good on his promise, what he needed to do was focus on the present.

So, smiling up at him, she gripped his hand more tightly and together they walked up the steps towards their hosts.

Emily Dunmore was as delightful as her husband, and Daisy quickly forgot the grandeur of her surroundings.

'James tells me that you met Rollo at his office?'

They were having coffee in the sun-soaked garden behind the main house.

'I did.' Daisy smiled at the older woman. 'I was waitressing at one of his parties.'

'I was working as a hotel receptionist when I met James. He was a guest, and I thought he was the most handsome man I'd ever seen.' Emily glanced across at her husband, her eyes gleaming. '*And* the most objectionable!'

Everyone burst out laughing.

'He kept extending his stay. Every day, another night. Only he wouldn't look me in the eye when he talked to me. And he was so officious. I was spitting mad.'

Shaking his head, James leaned over and took his wife's hand. 'I was only supposed to stay one night, but I couldn't take my eyes off her. I knew she was the one. Only I'd hardly even spoken to a woman outside of my family, and this goddess at the front desk clearly thought I was repulsive. So I thought I'd try and impress her with my natural authority.'

He groaned.

Daisy laughed. 'What happened?'

'I made a complete fool of myself for ten days and then I left.'

'What?' Daisy frowned. 'Why didn't you ask her out?'

James shook his head. 'I was too scared. I walked out of that hotel and got on a bus and went two thousand miles across the country to San Francisco.'

'That's so far away...' Daisy said slowly.

His face creased. 'I didn't have a choice. My dad had got me a job working for a friend in the construction business. It was all set up.'

Emily's fingers tightened around her husband's hand. 'I thought I hated him. But I'd got used to having him around, and every time I looked up I thought he'd be there—only he wasn't.' The older woman glanced across at Daisy, sadness clouding her eyes. 'I must have cried for a week.'

James stared affectionately at his wife. 'I didn't

cry. I did something far worse. I resigned after five weeks. I got another bus and went all the way back across the country and walked into that hotel and got down on one knee. I couldn't speak, I was so choked up—'

'But I knew what he was asking, and I was so happy I burst into tears.'

There were tears in Daisy's eyes too. But, glancing over at Rollo, she felt her body stiffen. He alone was dry-eyed, and there was a strange expression on his face she couldn't interpret.

Later, after lunch, the Dunmores retired, claiming tiredness and old age. But Daisy suspected it was their way of giving their young guests some space. Or maybe they still liked spending time alone, she thought wistfully as she and Rollo stretched out on the pristine white sand of the estate's private beach.

'It's so beautiful, isn't it?' she said softly.

A light breeze was blowing in across the ocean, and behind them clumps of grass quivered on the dunes beneath the hot afternoon sun.

He shrugged. 'It's not as beautiful as you.'

Daisy punched him lightly on the arm. 'We're alone now. You don't have to say that,' she said teasingly.

'I know,' he said quietly. 'But I mean it. You *are* beautiful.'

She looked up at him uncertainly. With the sun's dazzle illuminating the bones beneath his smooth golden skin, *he* was the beautiful one. But it wasn't his beauty that was occupying her thoughts. It was the slight distance in his manner. Remembering how he'd been before their lunch with James Dunmore, she nudged his arm again.

'And you're clever.' She gave him a quick reassuring smile. 'That's why tomorrow you're going to be the new owner of a prime piece of Manhattan real estate. And you'll have kept your promise to your father.'

His gaze was fixed on the ocean and her eyes fluttered anxiously over his face.

'You don't seem very happy.'

He turned to look at her, his mouth twisting into a smile. 'Of course I am. It's everything I want.'

Daisy nodded, her lips curving automatically into an answering smile. But inside a splinter of misery seemed to split her in two.

It's everything I want.

His words reverberated dully inside her head, blocking out the sound of the waves and the sudden swift beating of her heart.

It was just a throwaway remark. He probably hadn't given it a thought. But did that make it less or more true? And what had she expected him to say? That he had everything he wanted but *her*?

As casually as she could, she glanced past him out to sea. Really though, she was furtively watching his face. Since he'd confided in her she'd been doing that a lot, her eyes involuntarily searching for some change to reflect what felt like an incredible turning point in their relationship.

But what had really changed between them?

Sighing, she sifted through her memories, trying to be objective. It was true he'd shared a painful and personal fragment of his life, and for a short while at least he had seemed to need her. Not as an actress. Not for sex. But for herself.

And it had felt incredible at the time—a tiny but significant step towards trust, as though a tiger had momentarily allowed itself to be stroked.

Picking up a smooth white pebble, she sighed and laid it gently on the sand.

Of course, that was only her perception of what had happened. As far as Rollo was concerned he'd probably filed it away under 'momentary weaknesses, never to be repeated.' Certainly he'd given her no reason to think it had changed his view of either her or their relationship. Nor had he made any reference to their conversation or attempted to confide in her further.

She picked up another pebble. Whatever she thought had happened had most likely only taken place inside her head.

She sighed again.

'That's it. You're out!'

Startled, she glanced up as his fingers caught hers and firmly unclenched her hand, tipping the pebble onto the sand.

'Out of what?'

'The game. You had three strikes.' He frowned, his eyes picking over her face. 'Or in your case, three sighs! So come on—what's bothering you?'

It was the perfect opportunity to tell him the truth. That she loved him with a love that was rooted so deeply nothing could cause it to wither. That she would always have his back and would willingly go into battle for him.

But before she could reply he said quickly, 'Is it coming here? Meeting Emily?'

His eyes were startlingly green in the sunlight, his voice brusque with that anger again, and she felt her spine stiffen and the words dry in her mouth. For a moment there was no sound but the surf and the crooning cry of a distant gull, and then his fingers tightened on hers.

'Sorry.' He shook his head. 'I'm sorry. I didn't mean that to sound so forceful.' His mouth twisted. 'I know this is hard for you. James and Emily are good people, and I know how much you like them.'

Reaching into the sand, he picked up a pebble and handed it to her.

She nodded. 'They're so generous and humble. And so in love still.' Her heart gave a thump as he handed her another pebble. 'I suppose they remind me of my mum and dad.'

Shifting in the sand, she glanced over her shoulder to where the mansion could just be seen behind the sand dunes.

'Although Swan Creek is slightly bigger than the Love Shack.'

'More Love Chateau?' he said softly.

She smiled, responding to the teasing note in his voice. 'That's good. Perhaps you should try running a business.'

'I would love to run my own business, but I have this girlfriend. She takes up all my time.' Abruptly his face shifted, grew serious. 'How are they like your parents?'

His question pulled her up short. She frowned.

'I suppose they have the same sort of closeness...
like they're always aware of each other.'

She bit her lip. It was the sort of closeness she'd
dreamed about for years. A closeness born of trust
and honesty.

'That's a *good* thing, isn't it?'

He sounded so unsure that she burst out laughing. 'I think it is.'

He nodded. 'Only you sounded like it might not
be.'

His eyes searched her face so intently that suddenly she felt shy, self-conscious.

She shrugged. 'It's what I've always wanted.'
She gave him a swift, tight smile. 'But you can't
always get what you want—'

'Just what you need?'

Their eyes met.

I need you, she thought helplessly.

Instead she nodded. 'Which is why you can buy
chocolate and stationery everywhere.'

He groaned. 'Chocolate, I get. But stationery?'

She laughed. 'I love notebooks. And pens.'

'That stops as soon as we're married.'

'Is that your version of a prenup?' She raised an
eyebrow. 'Then you're going to need a lawyer, because stationery is non-negotiable.'

His eyes gleamed. 'In that case I might have a few non-negotiables of my own.'

Watching his expression grow blunt and tight, she shook her head. 'You have a one-track mind, Rollo Fleming.'

'Only with you. And if we weren't being forced into a state of celibacy—'

'It's only been a couple of hours.'

Glancing at his watch, he grinned. 'Five hours and seventeen minutes.'

It was stupid, but the fact that he was counting the minutes made her feel ridiculously happy. The urge to tell him so was almost overwhelming. But instead she shook her head.

'Only another day to go and then we'll be back at the apartment and we can do whatever we want, wherever we want.'

He ran his finger slowly down her arm. 'I thought *I* was the cold-blooded one,' he said softly.

She hesitated, and then took a breath, fear and hope tangling inside her. 'Of course, you could just tell James the truth. About why you want the building.'

He didn't reply—just stared past her at the tumbling waves so that she thought he hadn't heard her.

Finally he turned and gave her a small, polite smile. 'I don't think that will work.'

'Why not?' There was a knot in her stomach. Biting her lip, she tried to keep her voice steady. 'He wants to sell to someone with family values. You only want that building to keep a promise to your father.'

He was still smiling, but his fingers felt suddenly rigid against her skin. 'And how do I explain us? What "family values" does our sham engagement represent?'

There was no easy way to answer that.

She drew in a deep breath. 'It was just an idea.'

'Are you having second thoughts?'

His eyes on hers were dark and tormented. She shook her head, bewildered by the sudden shift in his manner. 'Of course not. I like the Dunmores, and I don't like lying to them. But my loyalty's with you, Rollo. It will always be.'

He nodded, and some of the tension in him eased. '*Always* as in *for ever*?'

She nodded. 'I know how much this deal means to you.'

She stared at him, blindsided by longing and hope and fear, wanting to speak, to go further, to risk everything. But instead she wrapped her fingers more tightly around his and squeezed.

'It means a lot to me too.'

She swallowed; her voice was shaking, and the beating of her heart was drowning out the sound of the waves. Only it didn't matter. All that mattered was finding the words to reach him. To make him understand. Even if that meant making herself vulnerable.

'I care about you and I want you to be happy.'

His face was blank and unsmiling. She held her breath as he stared at her in silence, and then finally he said quietly, 'I want you to be happy too.'

She could hear the struggle in his voice. But she knew how far they had come for him to admit even that much. And right now it was enough. Glancing down at the heart of pebbles she'd made in the sand, she breathed out softly. She had enough love for both of them.

'In that case let's go back to our room. We've got at least an hour before dinner.'

His dark, hungry gaze fixed on her face, tugging at her like a fish hook, so that suddenly she was breathless with desire, her body impossibly hot and tight. And then, without warning, he pulled her to her feet and hand in hand they ran towards the dunes.

The following morning, James Dunmore invited Rollo to his study to go over the proposal, and Daisy joined Emily on a guided tour of the estate's lavish gardens.

'So is this the actual creek?'

They were standing on a small wooden bridge above a grass-edged stream.

Emily smiled. 'It is. And those are the swans.'

As Daisy turned two immaculate swans glided across the water, their curving necks as delicate as white bone china cup handles.

'They were here when we bought the land. Just the two of them and a tiny run-down fisherman's hut.'

'How do you know they're the same pair?' Daisy asked curiously.

'The local wildfowl centre keeps track of the birds. And, of course, swans mate for life.'

Daisy nodded, a pang of guilt clutching at her stomach. It felt wrong to deceive such good people. But she had promised to be loyal to Rollo and she would keep her promise.

They had lunch behind the house, beneath a beautiful canopy of the palest purple wisteria.

'Emily and I thought we should have champagne.' James smiled at his wife. 'To celebrate your engagement.'

'How lovely!' Daisy managed to say. But she couldn't keep her eyes from sliding towards Rollo.

'That's very kind of you both.' His smile was dazzling and irresistible, and she forced her lips upwards into a smile of her own.

'I wonder, James, would it be premature to celebrate another forthcoming union?' Rollo spoke easily, master of the situation. 'Between our two companies?'

There was a short silence, and then James nodded slowly. 'Yes. Let's make it a double celebration.'

So that was it, then, Daisy thought dully. Everything she and Rollo had worked so hard to make happen had happened. Why, then, did she feel as though it was over before it had begun?

Suddenly she wanted to cry. But instead she smiled and laughed and drank champagne and ate her meal, focusing on every mouthful until finally it was over.

She lay down her spoon and looked up at her hostess. 'That was delicious, Emily. Thank you.'

Emily smiled. 'I think we'll take coffee in the gazebo. It's so hot, and there's always a lovely light breeze there.'

Five minutes later, James handed Daisy a cup of coffee, a smile creasing his face. 'You must come and stay with us after the wedding.'

They had moved to the gazebo and, as Emily had predicted, it was cooler and more comfortable to sit there, with the breeze coming in from the ocean.

'Rollo's looked at buying a property out here before, and New York's no place to bring up a family.'

A family!

Daisy nodded mechanically. But her mind was blank. They had never discussed a family, and she had no idea of the correct response.

But rolling her eyes at her husband, Emily leaned forward and said quickly, 'James! They're not even married yet!' She turned to Daisy. 'I'm sure you and Rollo will want to enjoy some time together in the city.'

James frowned. 'Of course.' He glanced apologetically at Daisy. 'I'm sorry. Forgive me, I'm an old man, I work on a different time scale to you and Rollo.'

Daisy nodded. The effort of smiling was making her face ache. 'P-please don't apologise. It's just we've never talked about children. We didn't have to...I mean, we won't be—'

She glanced across at Rollo, expecting him to smooth over her confusion. But he said nothing—just stared at her, an expression on his face she couldn't fathom.

There was a short, strained silence, and then Rollo cleared his throat.

Daisy's eyes were pleading with him. She needed his help—needed him to step up and save the day. Save the deal that was the culmination of years of hard work.

He'd never wanted anything more.

But now that it was within his grasp he realised that it wasn't worth the sacrifice. Wasn't worth the lies and deceit. And the compromise.

'We haven't discussed children.'

'Of course not. Couples these days tend to wait—' Emily began.

But he shook his head. 'I wish that were the reason, Emily.' He paused, his face like stone. 'But it's not. Daisy and I didn't discuss children because it's not you, James, who's working on a different time scale. It's me.'

His eyes met Daisy's and suddenly she knew what he was about to do.

'No, Rollo—'

Reaching over, he took her hand and squeezed it, his eyes greener and brighter than she had ever seen them.

'It never would have worked.'

Abruptly he dropped her hand and, standing up, he turned towards James, his face fierce.

'It's not her fault. I made her do it.'

'I don't understand, Rollo.' The older man stood up too. 'What time scale? And what did you make Daisy do?'

But he *did* understand, Daisy thought miserably. She could see it in the way his jaw was tightening, and in the hardening of his eyes.

'It's a fake. *We're* a fake.'

Even though she'd known what he was about to say, Daisy flinched at Rollo's choice of words. But it wasn't just what he said that hurt. The relief in his voice was so painful to hear that she had to grip the arms of her chair to stop herself from crying out loud.

'You'd do this? You'd lie about a marriage? About

being in love?' James shook his head, anger vying with disbelief.

Rollo shrugged. 'You wouldn't sell to me so I became someone else. And I needed Daisy to help me. To be my wife.'

She swallowed, the sound echoing inside her head. His eyes were staring at hers directly, as though they were alone, and the intimacy of his gaze was so at odds with the brutality of what he was saying that she thought she might throw up.

'How long were you going to carry on with this charade?' James asked coldly.

Rollo stared past him. 'A year,' he said finally. 'But I see now that a year was too long. Even a month has been too big a sacrifice to make.'

She breathed in sharply. It felt as if she'd been stabbed.

'You've gone too far, Rollo.'

James looked shocked, and for some reason that made everything so much worse.

'The deal is off. Over.'

Rollo nodded. For what felt like a lifetime he stood and stared at her, his gaze clear and calm, with the same acceptance of a gladiator stepping into the Colosseum. Then, turning, he walked away, his footsteps swift and light against the stone slabs.

'Please…' Daisy turned towards the Dunmores. 'You have to stop him. I know we did a bad thing, but he did it for the right reasons.'

James Dunmore stared at her in bewilderment. 'I don't understand. He made you a part of this, and yet you want to help him.'

'Yes, I do.' Her voice was filling with tears.

'But why?'

'I know why.'

Stepping forward, Emily Dunmore took Daisy's hand.

'It's because you love him, isn't it?'

'Yes, I do. But it doesn't matter anymore, does it?'

And as Emily pulled her into her arms she gave in to the misery and the pain and wept.

CHAPTER ELEVEN

FOUR WEEKS LATER, Daisy was still not entirely sure how she'd got back to New York. After Rollo had walked out, the Dunmores had refused to blame her for her part in the deception, and she had managed to stay calm while James had teased the whole story from her.

But in the face of their kindness, she hadn't been able to stop herself from bursting into tears again.

And it had been a relief to cry.

To grieve for what might have been.

But it had been more of a relief to get home.

For the first few days—a week, even—she had wept just like Emily Dunmore had. Then finally the tears had stopped.

Maybe she had no more tears left, she thought as she wiped down the tables in her parents' restaurant with swift, automatic efficiency. Or, more likely, the time for crying was over.

Now it was time to start living again. That was pretty much what David had said to her. She had visited him in rehab and told him the truth. And, just as she had done when he'd admitted his gambling problem, he'd pulled her into his arms and told her he'd be there for her.

Back at home, her father had handed her an apron and suggested she take a few shifts at the restaurant. Neither he nor her mother had pressed her for details. They'd simply welcomed her home and offered comfort and support.

And, of course, a job.

Glancing across the restaurant, Daisy almost smiled. Unbelievably, and for the first time in her life, she was actually enjoying waitressing. There was something comforting in the repetition of clearing tables, taking orders and making small talk with people. Better still it was nothing like her life in Manhattan.

It was a month since James Dunmore's limousine had dropped her at her parents' house. A month since she had last seen or spoken to Rollo. Not that she'd expected to hear from him. She'd known the minute he'd turned and walked away that she would be deleted from his life. And so she'd done the same, ruthlessly weeding out everything he'd ever given her.

Her heartbeat leapfrogged. She had given her

ring to James and he had promised to return it to Rollo. Given their history, she hadn't wanted there to be any risk of confusion. Or even the slightest possibility that she might have to see him again.

Although there was no chance of that happening. In his own words, the month they'd spent together had been a month too long.

The pain caught her off guard and, lifting up the condiments, she ran her cloth over the mustard and ketchup bottles, grateful for the distraction of physical activity.

Not that she was going to give in to the pain. She was stronger now. Sadder too. But determined to make her life matter. Which was why, when she'd saved up enough money, she was going to university to study English. She'd always wanted to go to university but had never thought she was good enough, and being an actress had been a legitimate way to disguise that self-doubt.

But she was done with being other people. Now she was going to be herself, and if that meant failing and facing up to her fears, then so be it. There was no shame in trying hard or finding something a challenge. Only in lying to others and oneself.

Her lips curved upwards. It wasn't quite a smile—she wasn't there yet—but maybe when

David came home tomorrow she'd be ready. Although, knowing her twin, he'd probably already guessed. After all, he knew her better than anyone. As well as he knew himself.

And just like that, her head began to spin, her words raising a memory of another restaurant, a pair of green eyes, and a deeper voice than her own saying softly, *'You're different. I know you as well as I know myself.'*

'Are we done here, Daisy?'

She jerked her head up, heart pounding. Her dad was standing in the doorway.

Outside in the street, the traffic lights had changed to green and cars were streaming over the crossroads and somehow it soothed her. Life carried on; her life too, and it was a good life. She had a loving family, a job and now she had a future.

Turning towards her father, she nodded. 'Yeah, I'm done. Let's go home.'

'What time is David getting here again?'

Daisy groaned. 'I told you, Mom. He doesn't need a lift. He wants to get a cab.'

Her mom frowned. 'And you think that's okay?'

'Of course. He caught a train from New York. I think he can manage a ten-minute cab ride.'

Her mother's face cleared. 'In that case I'm going to nip across to Sarah's to borrow her square tin. Then I can make the cake and you can ice it.'

Two hours later, Daisy was sitting at the table in her parents' backyard, trying to ice a message onto the top of her brother's favourite triple-layered chocolate-mousse cake.

He wasn't due home for at least an hour. Which was lucky, she thought seconds later as, glancing down, she saw that she'd made the letters far too big, so there was only room to fit 'Welcome Ho' across the top of the cake.

She sighed. Why was she doing the icing anyway? Her skill set in the kitchen was pretty much limited to peeling and slicing.

Dropping the icing bag, she looked up towards the kitchen window. 'Mom! *Mom!*' she yelled. 'I think you should do this. Otherwise it's just going to be a mess!'

From somewhere inside the house, she heard the doorbell ring and, rolling her eyes, she cursed softly. *Great!* It was probably Sarah. Now her mom would chat for hours and then it would be all

Daisy's fault when the cake looked as if it had been iced by a hyperactive five-year-old.

Except it wasn't a woman speaking. It was a man. Her body stilled. And, judging by the excitement in her mother's voice, it was not just *any* man. It was her brother. Damn, David! It was so typical of him to arrive early.

But suddenly she was grinning, her face splitting from ear to ear, and, jumping to her feet, she ran up the steps towards the house.

And stopped.

It wasn't David walking slowly across the deck.

It was Rollo.

Time had numbed her pain. But now it returned, more acute and intense than ever, together with a panic that seeped over her like melted tar, gluing her body to the spot.

'Hi.'

At the sound of his voice her skin seemed to shrivel over her bones. It was the voice she heard at night when she slept, and in daytime whenever her mind was idle.

It was a voice she'd learnt to love. A voice that made her want to run and never stop running.

'How did you find out where I lived?'

Her heart was turning over and over in her chest

like one of those mechanical toy monkeys. She wanted to touch him so badly it hurt. To reach out and caress that beautiful face. To hold him close and listen to him breathe. Only she couldn't. He wasn't hers to touch or caress or hold. He never had been.

'I asked David.'

His eyes were fixed on hers, and the expression on his face was nothing like his usual cool self-assurance. He looked hesitant, uncertain, like a man dying of thirst who thought he was seeing water for the first time in days.

She shook her head in shock. 'I don't believe you.' The thought of David betraying her hurt almost as much as Rollo's sudden reappearance in her life. 'He wouldn't do that.'

'I didn't give him a choice.'

Anger surged through, washing away the hurt and fear. She stepped towards him, fists curling. 'What did you do? Did you threaten him?'

'No. Of course not.'

'Why "of course"? That's what you *do*, isn't it?'

He ran a hand over his face and for the first time she noticed the dark shadows under his eyes, the slight hollowness in his cheeks. But she stonewalled the flicker of concern, watching in silence as he struggled for control.

'I just told him I needed to see you,' he said finally.

She stared at him, eyes widening with disbelief. 'You're joking, right? He knows what you did. He knows you blackmailed and humiliated and abandoned me. He wouldn't want you anywhere near me.'

Tears filled her throat and for a moment she couldn't speak, couldn't even look at him. But, no matter how hurt she was inside, she wasn't going to let herself fall apart in front of Rollo Fleming.

'Get out of this yard and stay away from me. And stay away from my family.'

'Daisy, please. I want—'

She flinched at the rawness in his voice. But as he took a step towards her she backed away, her hand raised up like a shield.

'It doesn't matter what you want, Rollo. I can't give it to you. Don't you understand? There's nothing left. Before I met you, I had a home and a job. It was only a room in my brother's apartment and a job I hated, but it was mine. It was *my* life. And you forced me to give it all up.'

She was fighting to breathe and, despite the heat

of the day, she felt cold—icy cold. And so alone. Just seeing him again reminded her of the pain of his absence. Of how badly she missed him.

She stared at his face. His beauty broke her heart.

Or it would have done if he hadn't already broken it.

Crossing her arms in front of her chest, trying to contain the pain and the misery, she lifted her chin. 'I gave you my loyalty and you told me it was worthless. You said being with me was a sacrifice you weren't prepared to make.'

'That's not what I meant.' He shook his head, his eyes suddenly too bright, his voice strained. 'I wasn't talking about my sacrifice. I was talking about yours.'

His shoulders rose and fell.

'What do you mean?' she said shakily.

'When you told me at the apartment that I didn't need to blackmail you...that you would help me get the building...I knew you meant it. I knew you'd be there for me.'

'So why did you throw it all away, then?' she stormed at him. 'We were drinking champagne. Celebrating our engagement and your deal. And then you told James it was all a sham.'

She bit her lip. Even though fury burned like fire

beneath her skin, she couldn't stop herself from caring about him. About the promise he'd made and now irretrievably broken.

Some of her anger faded. 'I'm sorry you lost the building.'

'You're *sorry*?' He frowned, his mouth twisting. 'How? Why?'

She looked past him, trying to sift through the tangle of her emotions to something neutral.

'I know how much it meant to you.'

He nodded, his face distant and shadowed. 'It's what I wanted my whole life. But it doesn't matter anymore.'

With an effort, she forced herself to sound cool, pragmatic. 'You did your best.'

His head jerked up, and the air seemed to tremble around him.

'You don't understand. I don't care about the deal. I don't care about the building or about the promise I made. I care about *you*.'

Her heart lurched, and beneath her feet the ground seemed to lurch too.

'No. You don't get to say that. Not here, not now.'

The tears she had been trying to hold back began to fall and angrily she wiped her face.

'I'm not crying because I care,' she managed finally. 'So don't think I am. I'm crying because I'm angry. With you.'

'I know. And you have every right to be angry. I treated you so badly.' His voice cracked and he breathed out raggedly. 'I wish I could go back and stop myself behaving like that.'

'You hurt me,' she raged at him. 'Humiliated me. Discarded me like I was last year's overcoat. You didn't just walk out on your deal. You walked out on me. You left me—'

Suddenly she couldn't bear it any more. She wanted him gone.

'Just go, Rollo, please.'

He shook his head. 'I can't.'

'Why not? Why did you even come here, anyway?'

He reached into his pocket, fumbling inside, and then suddenly she blinked, a flash of gold and green momentarily blinding her.

'Where did you get that?

It was the ring he had given her. The ring she had returned.

'From James. He came to see me. He gave it to me. He also gave me a pretty hard time. Told me a few home truths.' His face was drawn. 'I deserved them.' He drew a steadying breath. 'He told me I was a fool for letting you go. That you stood up for me after I left.'

Her cheeks grew warm, and she looked away. 'I did. Which makes *me* the fool, not you.'

'Daisy…'

He spoke quietly, but something in his voice tugged at her heart and she turned reluctantly, her pulse leaping frantically in her throat.

'He said you loved me.'

There was a moment of silence.

'Was that true?'

His skin was stretched tight across his cheekbones.

A shiver passed through her, but she couldn't lie to Rollo—no matter how much it hurt to tell the truth.

She nodded mutely.

'And what about now? Is it still true now?'

His eyes bored into her, reaching inside so there was nowhere to hide.

She nodded again.

His chest heaved, and he breathed out shakily. 'Then marry me.'

His voice was so quiet she could barely hear him. But his words punctured her skin like nails.

She stared at him numbly, her brain frozen. 'You

don't want to marry me, Rollo. You never did. I was just a means to an end.'

'At the start.'

His eyes were feverish and she could see that he was trembling, his whole body shaking like a marathon runner.

'But then it changed. *I* changed. Only I didn't know how to tell you.'

His face was tight with emotion.

'Tell me what?' she whispered.

'That I love you,' he said hoarsely.

And the last of her grief and pain was forgotten.

'I don't deserve you, Daisy. But I love you. And I want you to be my wife. For real, this time. That's why I had to leave. I knew you hated lying to the Dunmores. But you would have kept doing it—for me. And I couldn't bear that, so I had no choice. Or rather, I *had* a choice. And I chose you.'

Her heart tumbled over in her chest and a wild, dizzying happiness that was tinged with sadness swelled inside her.

'It was your dream. You gave up your dream for me.'

He shook his head.

'My dream's right here.'

Reaching out, he took her hands.

'And I have a confession. You were right. After I told James about my father he agreed to sell to me. We signed the contracts this morning. That's why I couldn't come before. I wanted there to be no confusion about why I want you to be my wife.'

His expression was so earnest, so eager, that Daisy couldn't decide if she wanted to laugh or cry. 'So I'm just a bonus?'

He laughed unsteadily. 'I'd say yes, but that icing bag looks dangerous!'

She smiled. 'In my hands it's a lethal weapon. Take a look at the cake if you don't believe me.'

His face shifted, grew serious. 'You're not a bonus, Daisy. You're the jackpot. I love you so much. I'll always love you.'

'*Always* as in *for ever*?' she said shakily.

Nodding, he gently lifted up her hand and slid the ring onto her finger.

For a moment they stared at one another in silence, like survivors from a storm. Then, fiercely, he pulled her against him, burying his face in her hair, his breath warm and shaky against her throat.

'I was so scared,' he whispered.

Gently, she stroked his cheek.

'Of what?'

'That James had got it wrong. That maybe you wouldn't forgive me.'

Her heart swelled protectively. 'I was scared too. Scared I'd lost you.'

'That won't happen. It can't. You're part of me. The truest part.'

He held her gaze. The emotion in his eyes was raw, naked, unguarded; and she loved him more than ever for being able to show his vulnerability and need for her.

She rested her cheek against his, soaking in his love. Finally, she sighed.

'We should probably tell my parents what's going on. They must be freaking out by now.' She frowned. 'I wonder why they haven't come out-side...'

Rollo screwed up his face. 'That might be my fault. I may have been a little...*impassioned* when I was trying to explain myself. I haven't really done the whole parent thing in a long time.'

She bit her lip, a question forming in her mind. Only before she could ask it he pulled her close— so close that she could feel the beating of his heart.

'I've been so angry for so long. With my past. With my mother. You made me face that anger and face my fears. But—'

'You need to see your mother,' she said gently. 'And Rosamund.'

He nodded. 'Yes.'

'I'm glad.' Watching his beautiful mouth curve upwards, she smiled teasingly. 'I always wanted a sister.' Her fingers curled into his shirt. 'But nowhere near as much as I want you.'

And then she pulled him closer and they kissed, losing themselves in each other, in desire, and in longing and need and love.

EPILOGUE

'YOU ARE KEEPING an eye on the time, aren't you, Dad?' Taking one last look at her reflection in the full-length mirror, Daisy glanced anxiously at her father's face. 'I don't want to be late.'

Her father shook his head. 'You're not late.' He paused, his eyes softening. 'But even if you were, you'd be more than worth the wait. You look beautiful, Daisy. Truly lovely.'

She smiled. 'You're my *dad*, Dad! You're supposed to think that.'

'Yes, I am.' Leaning back against the sofa, her father smiled back at her. 'But that doesn't make it any less true. And if you don't believe me, wait until Rollo sees you.'

Picturing her husband-to-be's reaction, Daisy felt her skin grown warm. She knew just how he would look at her...the way his green eyes would narrow and darken. Her heart contracted. Last night he had stayed in Manhattan, and she had travelled to the Hamptons with the rest of the wedding party.

And even though it had been less than a day she missed him.

As though reading her thoughts, her father reached out and squeezed her hand. 'Not long to go,' he said quietly.

Daisy nodded. Her dad was right. In less than an hour, and exactly one year after they'd met in his office, she would become Mrs Daisy Fleming.

They had decided on a small, intimate ceremony on the beach at Swan Creek. Daisy had always loved the idea of being married barefoot, with just the sound of waves instead of music, but she'd expected Rollo to want some huge high-profile society wedding.

He'd been adamant. The wedding was not for show. Only those nearest and dearest to them would be invited: her parents and David, his mother and Rosamund, and, of course, the Dunmores. And now it was really happening.

She shivered with nervous excitement.

'Are you cold?' It was her father's turn to look anxious. 'Do you need a cardigan or something?'

Dropping her gaze to her elegant white silk slip dress, Daisy laughed. 'Honestly, Dad! I'm about to get married. I'm not going to wear a cardigan.' She rolled her eyes. 'It's not even cold.'

It wasn't. A light breeze was blowing in from the ocean, and even though it was early evening the air was pleasantly warm.

'Must be wedding nerves, then.' Her father spoke lightly, but there was a glimmer of concern in his eyes.

She shook her head. 'I've never been more certain of anything, Dad.'

And with good reason.

A lot had happened over the last year. In collaboration with James Dunmore, Rollo had renovated his old apartment block into modern but affordable family homes, and Daisy had successfully completed her first year at university. More important, though, he had worked hard to forgive his mother, and together he and Daisy had spent time getting to know her and Rosamund. They weren't quite a family yet, but there was love and the beginnings of trust.

Her father cleared his throat. 'You really love him,' he said quietly. 'And it is real, isn't it?'

She nodded. 'I do. And it is.'

As part of her resolution to live her life as honestly as possible, she had told her parents everything that had happened with Rollo. David too had admitted his gambling problems, and it had been hard for her mother and father to hear the truth. But after their initial shock their love and support had remained unchanged.

'Of course, I'm just your dad, so I've never believed anyone could deserve you.' He smiled. 'But I don't think I've ever a seen a man so in love.'

She nodded, her heart pounding, suddenly overwhelmed by emotion.

'Right, then!' Her dad stood up and held out the simple posy of white daisies she'd chosen as a bridal bouquet. 'Are you ready?'

In reply, she slipped her arm through his.

Outside, the sun was starting to set, lighting the sky with a pinkish-gold haze.

Rosamund, her bridesmaid, was waiting at the edge of the beach, eyes bright with tears. 'Oh, Daisy, you look beautiful.'

But there was only time for a quick hug and then they were walking over the dunes towards the sea.

And there Daisy stopped, covering her mouth with her hand.

In front of her, all across the sand, lanterns glowed in the fading light. Lanterns arranged in the shape of a daisy. And standing beside the minister, in the centre of the petals, was Rollo—so golden and handsome in his white shirt and cream linen trousers that she could hardly breathe with loving him so much.

As she walked towards him he stepped forward, and she saw the love in the eyes.

'You made it.'

His voice was hoarse with emotion, and as he took her hand, she realised he was shaking as much as she was.

'*We* made it,' she said softly.

Later, after they'd exchanged their vows and mingled with their guests, he took her by the hand and led her away. As they stood beside the ocean, his eyes fixed on hers so intently that suddenly her pulse was leaping like the waves.

'Are you happy?'

His hand brushed against her bare shoulder, and a surge of desire rippled inside her.

'I've never been happier,' she said truthfully.

He stepped closer, his other hand curving around her waist. 'I love you, Daisy.'

'I love you too,' she whispered. 'I always will.'

'*Always* as in *for ever*,' he said fiercely, and as she nodded he wrapped his arms around her and kissed her as the sun set slowly behind them.

* * * * *

If you enjoyed
BLACKMAILED DOWN THE AISLE
why not explore these other great reads
by Louise Fuller?

CLAIMING HIS WEDDING NIGHT
A DEAL SEALED BY PASSION
VOWS MADE IN SECRET

Available now!